EPICS

EPICS

a collection of translated artifacts compiled by

PROF. ARAN DAMON PHD

A WORD FROM THE AUTHOR

Deep within an abandoned silver mine, at an undisclosed location, in the very bowels of the Earth itself, it was there that I found the mammoth pile of copper tablets. Some were still whole, while others were broken, with their pieces either scattered about or lost. The etchings on some were as clear as day, while on others the writing had faded with time.

Carbon dating of the samples have not yielded consistent results, though the average seems to place them between 4500 BC and 3500 BC. The writing upon them is a complex cuneiform script, so I am tempted to place the tablets within the Uruk IV period in Sumer. Astoundingly, the pictographs bare complexities which were not prevalent until thousands of years later.

The effort to extract these tablets from their ancient resting place was exhausting, but when finally accomplished, stock was taken of them by my archaeological team. And what a prize!

Here, lost for millennia, was a work of art unlike any other in ancient history. There are people across the globe who claim to have discovered artifacts that are out of place in time. Most common are gears, and other small metal structures inside million year old pieces of coal.

While these tablets are themselves no different from any other copper-work of the era, the contents of the written story are impossibly sophisticated, and speak of technologies that had not yet even been conceived of in fiction until the latter part of the twentieth century.

My team and I know the tablets cannot be a hoax, for the mine had not seen use in the past six hundred years, and the chambers were undisturbed in all that time.

Even so, I realize that anyone in the scientific community or the public at large would think me a fool for publishing a scholarly collection of my findings. Doing so would jeopardize my grants and my professorship, and my name would be made into a laughing stock.

And yet, stunned by the enormity of the find, my team and I began the long and arduous translation of the tablets, which sometimes took us hours to decipher merely a single word.

After time, a picture of the grand story took shape.

Here was Barry Happypants and his quest to rid the Universe of the interplanetary tyrant, Gribulor, the Great Goat-Man.

Here was Barry's encounter with the unstoppable universal hero El Krunko, and how the two became a pair of legends to rival all legendary figures.

Here are the adventures of this Dynamic Duo throughout time and space, all the more marvelous thanks to their seemingly nonsensical nature.

Behold as they ally themselves with the eerie Ethnocentric Dracula to battle the malevolent Multinational Mummyman!

Marvel as they discover the text that tells the tale of El Krunko's past!

Be astounded as the very edges of chronology and geography are explored and burst apart!

Such are the wonders of this translation, that while I cannot risk my professional career, or the promising futures of my team, I would be wrought with regret if I were to never share the compilation. Thus, under a pseudonym to protect my identity, I have finally taken steps to publish this work.

I dedicate this compilation to you, dear reader,

and to all of humanity. It is a riveting tale, that if it indeed comes from the Uruk IV period, threatens to shatter the paradigm of belief we hold so sacred. Our understanding of the past, and indeed the Universe as a whole, is to be reshaped by this Epic tale, an impossible story from the depths of time itself.

But, the translation is not yet complete. Still a huge pile of undeciphered copper tablets remains stored under lock and key in our hidden warehouse. We hope to finish our grand task soon, and finally discover the ultimate fate of Barry Happypants and El Krunko!

Perhaps the sale of this compilation will further support our efforts, as our grant money has long since run dry.

Now, without further adieu, I present to you, Epics.

"With my eye on the future, and my heart in the past." – Prof. Aran Damon PhD Archaeology

A NOTE ON THE TRANSLATION

I must warn the reader that without a mastery of cuneiform and other pictograph base languages, true appreciation of the original script is impossible.

We apologize for not releasing images or pressings of the original script, but due to the varying size of the pictographs, as well as steep production costs, it is currently necessary for us to release a translation in the King's English only.

Serious scholarly requests for the original script from respectable academic sources will be addressed on a case by case basis.

The English translation contains no less than a 28% margin of error, as well as unusual writing artifacts. Syntax has been added by our language specialists in order to make the text flow in the left to right cohesive linear nature of English.

This is especially found in the addition of conjunctions and pronouns to the text, as well as careful interpretation of subtle variations in the original script to provide for adverbs and certain adjectives.

Some pictographs, despite our best efforts, remain entirely untranslatable. In order to provide insight into what the script might mean, we have used similar modern words inferred from meaning in the surrounding text.

The spelling of names and places are of particular concern. The phonetic sounding of the cuneiform does not allow for an exact pronunciation. Reasonable translations based off of well known words in similar languages have been used, and at times may vary.

Please understand that this is a limitation of language as a whole, and not the expertise of our translators. There are many ancient scripts which can be read, but not spoken. They are truly dead oral languages.

Of further note are the use of numbers and other mathematical symbols. Modern mathematics is base 10, while math in the script functions at a base of 8. Furthermore, while there are pictographs depicting specific numbers or formulas, there are also duplicate methods of representing numbers and figures.

For this reason there will be a variation of numbers that are spelled, and those which are depicted as numerals. Please note that this is not an error in the text, but a representation of the two types of mathematical scripts.

Numbers and formulas are written using standard mathematical symbols in a base 10 system, and we have done our best to ensure that they are presented correctly. On rare occasion, Roman numerals are used for an obscure, third variation of mathematics in cuneiform.

So as not to be mistaken for the normal presentation of numbers, tablets are individually numbered in Roman numerals. As the tablets were not numbered themselves, they are numbered for scholarly purposes in the organization of the linear narrative, and while we have done our best, may not always be in the correct intended order.

At times in the text you will find a series of 10 asterisks. This marker represents a vignette which appears multiple times in the original script. While not an engraving on the tablet itself, the vignette is a line of colored scorch marks. Analysis of the marks and their metallic residue indicates they were created with strips of burning magnesium.

As magnesium was not first isolated as an element until 1808, where it was discovered by a fellow

Englishman, chemist Sir Humphry Davy, this provides further confusion into the anachronism of the tablets themselves.

Carbon dating of the scorch marks indicate that they fall within the same time range as the bulk of the engravings, and were more than likely created at the same time, or shortly thereafter.

I lcavc it up to you, dear reader, to decide for yourself whether such oddities cause you to doubt the authenticity of the tablets, or whether they reinforce the mystery, and allow for the possibility that they are, in fact, as I believe them to be, genuine artifacts from antiquity.

– Prof. Aran Damon PhD Archaeology

TABLET: I

X = 1

* * * * * * * * * *

It was dark, too dark for the corporate special assassin to see from the position he was crouched in. 35, 34, 33, the seconds ticked away until he was supposed to spring on his mark. The seconds seemed like months as they rattled in the silent killer's head. He readied his weapon, when suddenly a loud whoosh sounded, and sparks appeared behind him. He turned, only to see a hairy, but well-dressed, Red Monkey step out from a vintage automobile.

"Beep-boop," went the parking alarm.

"What's going on here? Who are you?"

The primate smiled and extended his hand. "Greetings! My name is Good Good Gorilla Guy, and I've been sent to give you a hand, Barry Happypants!"

"Oh... Good," Barry replied, for that was the corporate special assassin's true name. "See those diplomats below?" He turned and gestured. "They're our targets. Now urk– "

The tip of a silvery steel blade burst out from the middle of his chest. Barry Happypants collapsed, quite dead.

The Red Monkey removed the Sword of Epic Conquest from the assassin's chest, and wiped it clean. "Now, for El Krunko!" he cried in joy, and hopped back into his car.

TABLET: II

* * * * * * * * *

Bob the Martyr walked towards a town of Green Pig men. Upon his entrance, he was laughed at by all, for he was neither green nor a pig...

When without warning, everyone fell silent. Far in the distance a cloud of dust had appeared in the air, and it seemed to be getting closer. In the coattails of the strange dust-storm there arose a maniacal laughter that was getting louder and louder.

Cassandra the Rotten, the leper prophetess, stumbled out of her cathedral and addressed the town. "Dark tidings! The ends of the world! Foul death on the wings of a Chevy '67! Poison! Horror! Ahhhhhh!!!!" She pulled at her hair, and bits of flesh oozed off her bones.

Langust, the Mayor of the town, had the guards remove her from the scene, and soon, the car pulled up. A finely dressed monkey leaned out the window and spoke aloud, "Hey Bob... Where's your brother, The Gimp Boy?"

Bob pointed across the plains, to the south, and as quickly as the mysterious stranger had come, he was gone.

Mean Mean Monkey Man soon arrived at a small clay hovel. After hopping out of his ride, he pushed aside the pig-hide drapes, and fell into a manic fit of laughter. "Surely not this, pathetic creature! You cannot be the Lord of the Slay? Not this!"

El Krunko, The Gimp Boy, rolled out of his eatin-sack, and snorted at the trespasser.

TABLET: III

"Bwa ha ha ha!" Mean Mean Monkey Man cackled.

El Krunko looked up confused, still half encased in his sack, his chin and lips shiny with chicken grease. "Huh? Who're you?"

Mean Mean Monkey Man leapt across the room before El Krunko could react, and grabbed The Gimp Boy's Ancestral Chainsaw!

"Hey! That's mine!" El Krunko protested, but M.M.M.M. ignored him, and he fired the power tool up. With one swing of the device he severed El Krunko's left pinky toe. "Ouch! Quit it!" El Krunko whined. "I'm not supposed to fight after eating, it gives me cramps!"

But M.M.M.M. was merciless. He continued swinging the chainsaw wildly, seeking to end the life of El Krunko with the very gift of his ancestors, the ones who gave him life! Oh, the irony!

But El Krunko, even when he was young, was a swift and superior warrior. He dodged every blow as he waited for his opportunity to strike. Finally M.M.M.M. left his flank open, and El Krunko gave him a powerful left hook. Kapoweey! The A.C. flew from the primate's hands and embedded itself in the clay wall of the hovel, where it vibrated maniacally like a crazy kid with epilepsy. Cracks spread outward from where it had struck.

"Oh no!" El Krunko cried. "My house!"

While El Krunko panicked and tried to loosen the chainsaw, it dawned on M.M.M.M. how his evil plans could come to fruition. He scooped up El Krunko's severed toe and exclaimed, "Goodbye for now, El Krunko! When we meet again, it shall be your doom!" He raced out the door and sped away in his time travelin' car.

El Krunko finally wrenched the chainsaw loose, only to find with dismay that his hovel had crumbled to dust, and the mad monkey was nowhere to be seen. He scratched his head.

Suddenly, a Green Pig came racing towards him from the distance, panting and out of breath. "El Krunko!" he gasped. "Your brother Bob the Martyr is dead. Will you not take up his holy quest to rid the Universe of the Purple Aardvarks?"

Seeing as he had nothing better to do, El Krunko agreed.

TABLET: IV

* * * * * * * * * *

Page 1:

It was dark, too dark for the corporate special assassin to see from the position he was crouched in. 35, 34, 33, the seconds ticked away until he was supposed to spring on his mark. The seconds seemed like months as they rattled in the silent killer's head. He readied his weapon, and on the count of 3 he dropped from his perch, and fell upon the Purple Aardvark automated defense statue, and into the fray of diplomats.

TABLET: V

The diplomats scattered rapidly, too rapidly for a group of bureaucrats. They quickly threw off their cloaks, and from underneath drew the giant razor blade weapons traditional to the clan of the Rey-zore guards. It was a trap! Gribulor the Great Goat-Man knew he was coming! But how??

TABLET: VI

Our hero was now surrounded by bad guys with big sharp knives. It's a good thing that his weapon was a Buster Sword. And even though this sword was taller and wider than he was, he wielded it like an artist would a brush... And with it he painted a middle finger on the wall with the caption, "Eat my ass and balls Gribulor! - Love, Barry Happypants," in his fallen enemy's blood.

TABLET: VII

Without a moment to spare, Barry leapt out the nearest window as the statue's battle timer went off. A huge explosion wracked the top floor of the Aardvark Royal Assembly and he fell into his well placed Red Monkey Mech-Armor cockpit, where he immediately jammed it into overdrive.

They knew I was coming, he thought, *which can only mean one of two things. Either that bitch in the fur salon was lying, or the mark of the Blood Prophet on my left testicle is a forgery!*

"Great Gribulor's Ghost!" he cried out in sheer terror.

TABLET: VIII

Knowing that Gribulor's vengeance would be

swift, merciless, quick, and without mercy; Barry gripped the control stick of his Mech-Armor and piloted it into space.

"Another day, Gribulor!" he cried out in frustration.

A few hours later, he stood in front of Ostegu Fur Salon. As he entered, the stench of cheap purrfume overwhelmed him. *She was here all right, but nowhere in sight. Cesta 5567-NR4W the pleasure cyborg could not be far.*

TABLET: IX

On any normal day the salon would be filled with cheap women and easy prostitutes, but today he could detect a hint of class in the place. Outraged by the fact Cesta would overstep her bounds and come to his side of the sex district, Barry drew his Buster Sword and vanquished many a rich man's mistress that fateful breakfast hour. Covered head to toe in blood, hair, and lipstick, he burst his way into the sacred chambers behind the easy chair. She was close. Almost too close. No, the illustrious lover to the mad but brilliantly evil Dr. Corpse Von Slaughterheim could not be far.

TABLET: X

Striding past the bed adorn with red crushed velvet sheets and silk covered pillows, Barry reached the wooden door that led to Von Slaughterheim's personal lovemaking chamber. He burst through the oak and sent splinters across the room. There sat Cesta beside the insane inventor of the Demon Ray, who calmly replaced his monocle to its standard position while Cesta's modesty and panic circuits fired. She cried out as she covered herself with the blanket.

"My quarrel is not with you, Doctor!" Barry proclaimed. "It is with the synthetic tart beside you!"

TABLET: XI

"Mind if I finish first?" the Doctor queried. Barry politely complied and exited the room, allowing the Doctor just enough time to complete the task at hand.

Barry re-entered the room a few seconds later, right as the Doctor was leaving. Unfortunately, Barry was blissfully unaware that Von Slaughterheim was, in fact, Gribulor's newly appointed Personal Assistant of Killing Innocent People, and his chance at apprehending the renowned criminal mastermind passed as quickly as the Doctor had finished.

Barry proceeded to kick Cesta in the face, tie her up, and repeatedly hit her in the head with the butt of his Buster Sword until she told him everything.

Two days earlier, she screwed some pig dude with a tattoo on his nuts.

TABLET: XII

Barry finally knew the grisly truth. His very own uncle (the only other Green Pig who could possibly have a mark of the Blood Prophet), was the mysterious unknown soldier fighting for the Purple Aardvarks, and had been a traitor to the Green Pigs all along!

Barry fumed with rage. Somehow that dim witted twerp had stumbled into a romantic encounter with Cesta. Barry drew his Buster Sword and chopped the robotic bitch in twain.

"Good riddens! To think of anyone else having sex with something that touched my uncle in his special place. I've done my good deed for the week!"

As Barry dropped to his knees and thought silently to himself about the inevitable upcoming carnage, a voice rang out over the loud speakers. "Dr. Slaughterheim has left the building."

"Shit!" Barry yelped. "The good doctor is my only hope."

TABLET: XIII

Barry soon found Von Slaughterheim powering up his intergalactic unicycle. "Doctor, my money's good. Give me a device to find my traitorous uncle."

"Follow me to my laboratory. There I shall sell you a device that seeks out the very soul of its target, and sucks that soul from its material form. Mwa ha ha ha ha ha ha!"

The Doctor threw his head back in manic laughter, but suddenly ceased, as if embarrassed, or realizing that he'd said too much. Barry narrowed his eyes and fired up his trustworthy lie detector. The needle was in the red!!

Barry unsheathed his Buster Sword... But it was too late.

TABLET: XIV

The invasion had already begun. Red Monkeys now dropped from the sky with packs on their back that let forth great numbers of explosives as they fell.

Explosions abounded, and in the concrete wind storm that ensued, the evil doctor made his escape into the night once again.

"I've gotta get outta here..." Barry calmly remarked. Alas, he came to the decision too late, for he had already run behind schedule. "Oh no!" he shouted when he looked at his watch. "I've missed the transport!"

Just then, a portal in space and time opened before him.

The aroma of sweet Brand Name Green Pig Perfume, the expensive gourmet type that hinted of roast chicken, misted out of the leery portal. He shrugged and dove right in.

The portal vanished behind him, and as the concrete dust settled, all that remained was a Buster Sword.

TABLET: XV

Now, a digression.

For those of you who are skeptical about the possibility of the spontaneous manifestation of space/time portals, or who even doubt their existence, remember Scienrontus' theorem: if space=a, and time=b, then $ab((a+b)/b)$ should yield the well known and hilarious mathematical rule of thumb.

Now that this argument has been exhausted and irrefutably proven, we rejoin Barry, who found himself in a strange place.

He sat in mud, surrounded by hogs that were pink instead of green. He tried speaking to one pig in the tongue of the Green Pig Men, but the creature did not appear to comprehend. "What manner of devilry is this?" Barry exclaimed.

TABLET: XVI

Perplexed by the strange dilemma of how he should go about rescuing his fellow pigs from this strange affliction, he grasped at his side, only to find his manner of attack missing.

"Great Gribulor's Ghost, now my Buster Sword's gone! Gribulor will pay for this magic spell he's cast upon me and my home planet!" Barry grabbed the nearest pink pig and cradled it in his arms sobbing. "Why!!!! I swear on this day that wherever I go, whomever I meet, whatever the situation, no matter where I am, I shall slay the Green Pig enemies in your name."

Barry kissed the pink pig on its brow with a melodramatic display of sympathy and tears in his eyes. "Now to find a suitable replacement for my weapon!"

"Oink."

TABLET: XVII

He left the wooden hutch that housed the pigs, still wracked with emotion. A short distance away he spied a brick house with smoke floating lazily from its chimney. He raced to the door and knocked. A buxom blonde with pigtails appeared in the opening. "Ja, can I be helpen you?" she asked in a strange accent.

Barry was taken aback. He cleared his throat and ran a hand through his hair. "Madame, I come in need of a weapon."

She reached behind the door and pulled a mighty battle axe from its resting place. "This axe is a family heirloom, passed through history until a mighty warrior could claim it. I see that you are this warrior." She handed the axe to the still astonished Barry.

TABLET: XVIII

Barry took the axe from her hands, and slyly turned away as he examined it.

"I was looking something more along the lines of... A SWORD!" And he decapitated her with it, casting a series of curses as he did so.

"May the worshipers of the Axe be met with a swift demise, and their bodies be eaten alive by monkeys!" Since Barry had once taken a Red Monkey oath to kill any axe-wielding fiends, he thus hated axe-wielders profusely, and rightly so. "Now to find a more suitable replacement for my weapon! Will the madness never cease!?!?"

TABLET: XIX

And so, Barry traveled the countryside in search of a good sword, slaying farmers and highwaymen as he went. After a few months and a brief bout with the guard of the (former) town of Villeville, he finally came across a seller of swords. "Good sir," Barry said. "Give me your finest blade." The seller did as Barry asked, and was promptly disemboweled. "Now to find a way out of this nonsensical land!"

"The land of Og is where you'll wantin' to be gettin' to," said a voice.

Barry looked above, and spied a tiny man garbed in green lounging in the bow of a tree.

TABLET: XX

"Noble tree spirit. Tell me wise one, where might I find the land of Og?"

The tiny green man puffed on his pipe, and pointed towards Barry with fervor. Before the man had a chance to say a word, Barry was off in a flash, following the direction of the man's pointed finger. "What a strange fellow. I was going to tell him to get off my mushrooms. The land of Og is a state of mind. Hope he doesn't go mad looking for a place that doesn't exist. Eh?" With a shrug, he went back to his pipe.

TABLET: XXI

Barry traveled day and night, stopping only to pleasure himself. Eventually he arrived in a quaint town. Thinking it to be in the land of Og, he stopped a citizen and made his demands. "Take me to your wisest man, citizen."

The kindly fellow led Barry to the home of Sokrabes, where Barry was given an audience with their eldest sage. Barry entered Sokrabes' solemnly sacred chamber. "Barry Happypants, we meet again!" Sokrabes was none other than Doctor Corpse Von Slaughterheim!

TABLET: XXII

"Eat my steel you wretch! Your soul stealing powers will never foul the land again." At this, Barry Happypants drew his finest blade (which was the only one he had), and swung ferociously at the Doctor, who, being the brilliantly mad fiend that he was, prepared himself for every situation... Except this one, for he was the *good* Doctor Corpse Von Slaughterheim, and not his *evil* clone. With many unkind sounds, Barry Happypants transformed the award winning scholar into a pile of muck and goo.

As Barry was painting his standard goodbye form letter on the wall, a team of droid defenders entered the room with presents, candy, and a large cake bearing the words, "Welcome Back Mr. Happypants!" writ on the top in purple frosting.

"Purple Frosting's my favorite!" Barry yelped out, as the droids dropped the welcoming party, and pointed their guns at the returning hero, who was drenched in their Master's corpse.

TABLET: XXIII

Barry could do nothing to stop them. He was soon knocked unconscious, and awoke hours later in a silvery hall. His hands were bound in adamantine wire, and his legs were trapped in a pair of straight-trousers.

"You have cost me my best adviser, but his death was worth this prize," boomed a familiar voice. Barry shook with fear, and raised his eyes to stare into the four red eyes of his sworn archenemy, Gribulor the Goat-Man! Gribulor raised his Devil Sword of Demon Death and swung, as if in slow-motion, at Barry's head. The sharp steel of the blade severed it clean from his body.

"Ha ha ha," Gribulor chuckled. "With your head and body on the opposite ends of the galaxy, you shall never be able to oppose me!" Barry's severed head wept in murderous rage.

TABLET: XXIV

It was dark, too dark for the corporate special assassin to see from the position he was crouched in. 35, 34, 33, the seconds ticked away until he was supposed to spring on his mark. The seconds seemed like months as they rattled in the silent killer's head. He readied his weapon, and on the count of 3 he dropped from his perch, and fell upon the Purple Aardvark automated defense statue, and into the fray of diplomats. *They scattered, fast. Too fast*, he thought.

As he leapt forward, bringing his blade upon the first of his enemies, he had the strangest feeling of deja vu. He slaughtered them in classic fashion, and took up his Buster Sword to write his calling card. This was when he just couldn't take it anymore. "I swear I've done this before!" he exclaimed, as he stopped writing and shook his head.

Just then a voice bellowed out from the sky. "I have transported you back in time to avenge my death. You must go east and find the orb of the drunken wanderer. Then you will understand."

"I understand!" Barry cried out, as he magically separated apart from his body (although he didn't notice it at the time), and wandered off toward the east in semi-transparentness.

TABLET: XXV

Barry reached the east. He realized this when he came across a giant silver E lying on the earth. Scanning the barren wasteland for signs of a drunk, he soon saw a teetering figure on the horizon. The Drunken Wanderer, however, had seen the ghostly

Barry as well. "Well-met stranger," the drunkard cried out, as he took a swig of his whiskey.

Barry charged and swung his blade, though it did nothing while in his incorporeal state. "Damnation. Give me your orb!"

"First you must answer my riddle. There is a well-known and hilarious mathematical formula that can be obtained through the variables of space and time. Recite to me the proper combination of variables, and you shall have my orb."

Barry's sense of deja-vu increased tenfold. Had he not just heard the very same equation a short while ago?

TABLET: XXVI

Barry's head swam with numbers and letters as he tried to recall the proper equation. "A + b no wait, b – a/c... No... Gimme a sec here... Is it a+b(ab/b)?" Upon speaking, the ground began to shake, and the sky began to thunder.

The Drunken Wanderer raised his whiskey bottle upon high and spoke. "You ignorant fool more foolish than the King of fools, who just so happens to be the most ignorant man in the Universe! You've spoken the great unspoken equation which must never be uttered! The disruption to the flow of the space time continuum can never be undone. Who knows what hideous damage has already taken place! The whole World Universe could be in peril most fierce!"

Barry entered his classic fighting pose. "Can the talk, meander man! Gimme the orb, or I'll say it again."

TABLET: XXVII

The Drunken Wanderer sighed. "It matters not. You could say it a hundred thousand times and the damage has already been done." With these words the man slumped to the ground to await his fate, but Barry would not give up so easily. Barry turned and ran in the direction from whence he'd come, but in his haste failed to see a large stone underfoot, and he tripped over it. He fell to the ground with a great thud, and was knocked unconscious.

When he awoke, he had the peculiar sensation of floating in thick liquid, as if he was back in the womb. When he opened his eyes and saw the prison chamber around him, he instantly realized the bone-chilling truth.

Gribulor had separated his head from his body, and shipped them to opposite ends of the galaxy.

TABLET: XXVIII

Barry instantaneously knew this, because the connection between his neural transmitters and the bio-mechanics in his neck were completely severed. "Great Kelzinger's Fellbanger! I've got to get my body back!" Barry's eyes darted back and forth across the room as he began to formulate a plan. He was surrounded by two thousand other mechano-glass tubes, each one of which contained the heads of other enemies of the monstrous Head of the Corporation. "This must be the Corporate Headquarters. Blast! If only I a head on my shoulders, I'd know what to do." (For he was not very intelligent, and he knew it very well).

Meanwhile, eight hundred thousand years

earlier at the exact same location, the Elder Porcupine in the Mammal Coalition was attempting to formulate a plan of his own. He shuffled his leafed portfolio across the tree-stump podium with a nervous twitch in his movement. Ever so calmly, he disguised the twitch as he adjusted his wormacle.

"Fellow trusted colleagues. As we all know, we face a dire dilemma. Do we decide to go with the first plan of–"

He was abruptly cut off as everyone's attention suddenly focused on the Monkey Diplomat. "It... It can't be!"

TABLET: XXIX

The Monkey Diplomat lay in a pool of his own bloody vomit. "Poisoned!" cried out the King of the Naked Mole Rats. The other mammal leaders eyed each other suspiciously, for they realized the Monkey Diplomat was the deciding vote for plan two, and now the first plan would surely win the count.

But the representative of the savage human race, Lothar Happypants, leapt to the front of the room and exclaimed, "Tis Lord Briguvor, of the Goat-Men, to blame!" A hush went through the crowd, but Briguvor was prevented from escaping, and was quickly brought to trial and executed in a painful manner involving a gallon of milk and a rubber hose. And from generation to generation, the Goat-Men hated the Happypants family, which explains the antagonism between Gribulor and Barry.

TABLET: XXX

The feud was horrific at times. The hatred of the Goat-Men by the Happypants family was passed on through generations, and grew stronger as the fighting raged on. As Barry's severed pig head lie still upon the tube's counter top, he recounted the legend in his head.

Many years ago, when the Goat People's milk still streamed plentifully from their nipples, Sacred Goat Cheese was aged under the glow of the rare Purple Sun. The hapless Ceril Happypants was tricked by Gribulor's ancestor to eat this forbidden cheese, and the curse of the green swine was forever instilled upon The Happypants family.

I will not let you down, Ceril! thought Barry. *I will smite the Goat People from existence once and for all, and undo this wretched wretchedness.*

TABLET: XXXI

Upon making that fateful promise, Barry activated the emergency detonators in his eyeballs. They separated from his eye sockets and attached themselves with a plop against the interior of the mechano-glass. Within seconds they exploded, and the mechano-glass support tube split into two equal pieces, and fell to the floor with a crash.

As the milky fluid drained away, Barry's tongue flicked open his fake tusk, and clicked on his jet pack. His neck roared with flames, and Barry took off towards the nearest airlock... and flew immediately into the nearest tube, for without eyeballs he was blind, and he knew not where he was going. The tube fell, and like a series of biological dominoes, created a chain effect whereby every tube in the chamber tipped and shattered.

"What have I done?! I've set free the Legendary Heads of State... Amongst others!" Within moments, the chambers filled with the roar of jet-packs, and the stench of afterburners.

TABLET: XXXII

It didn't take Barry long to enlist the help of a friendly pair of heads, and some months later found himself on the other side of the galaxy. A brief investigation found Barry's body at the beach, where it had been flirting with other headless bodies in string bikinis.

"Presto change-o!" Barry spoke the words of command, and his body and head was fused once more. Having no further need for the friendly heads, he squashed them underfoot like melons. But when he looked up, the crowds were fleeing the beach in terror, and Barry at once realized why...

A mile high wave of water was about to come crashing down upon them!

TABLET: XXXIII

Killing like he's never killed before, Barry was able to instantaneously erect a mile high wall of slaughtered beach goers. He felt like the supreme leader of beachfront defense, warding off any garbage that mother nature was able to throw at him. Thousands of elderly Higlorians cheered, because the wall of the dead saved their retirement housing. They still complained of being cold, however, despite the temperature being well into the millions.

"Three cheers for Barry Happypants!" they cried one and all, as they bestowed upon him a gift of great power.

TABLET: XXXIV

From this moment on, the mere mortal known as Barry Happypants was no more. The severe heat of Higloria, which was unknown to him at the time, for his head was inside a transparent head-sized spacecraft, had melted off all of his body's skin.

The Higlorians, not knowing that he was supposed to look like a Green Pig (as that was what he used to be before the Red Monkey High Priestess had transformed his endoskeleton into a complex nano-machine), used their magical skills to turn him into a Higlorian, head and all!

"Shit! What have you done!?" cried out Barry Happypants as he examined his feathered arms, and Higlorianesque razor-sharp claws.

"Higlorian Shell with a creamy metal filling is an ancient combination, oh holy one. Except for your memories, you are now the spitting image of our most worshiped God, Larry BappyMaps."

Barry was outraged. "The only reason I'm on this stinking planet in the first place is because of Gribulor. I *was* going to let you live, but now that you've..." And at this point Barry drew his newly acquired spiked scorpion tail up as he would a sword. "... RUINED my chances of regrowing my Green Pig exterior, you can kiss that mercy goodbye! Eat mechanized you death stupid aliens!!"

And upon saying this, Barry laid waste to the

entire remaining coastal population of Higlor. Fourteen days later, standing amidst the carnage in the shadows of Dead Man's Dam (as it later came to be called), Barry Happypants knelt to the ground and yelled to the sky. "Ye Gods above me! I must conceal my true identity in order to get to Gribulor. No longer am I Barry Happypants! From this day on I shall be known only as..."

TABLET: XXXV

"Happy Barrypants! And now, vengeance!" Happy used his mighty wings to fly to the planet of the Great Goat-Men, the name of which cannot be written here to protect copyright interests. He walked freely among the Goat-Men, thinking dark thoughts over many mugs of bitter ale. But his mind could not be dulled, could not be bent from its singular purpose: plotting the utter destruction of Gribulor.

Happy spent many sleepless nights and sunless days with his mind and brow furrowed under the weight of his planned revenge. People shuddered as he passed in the street. Children and midgets ran from his path. All somehow sensed the blackness that had poisoned his entire being. Flecks of spit made his chin shine, and he perpetually muttered under his breath like a lunatic. Yet suddenly, one day, his plan was finished, and Happy smiled a grim smile.

There's only one thing left to do...

TABLET: XXXVI

He had to have as much sex as possible, and wait for something to randomly happen. Happy put his plan immediately into motion, and when he was finished (which was signified by Happy lifting the goat woman above his head, driving his venomous tail thru her womb, and ripping her into two bloody uneven pieces), a piece of paper fell onto his head. On the paper was found writing which claimed Gribulor's personal driver was staying at, "The Hotel." This obviously meant that Gribulor was at The Hotel as well. Happy promptly ventured to the place, where he politely asked Peter, the customer service representative at the help desk, if he could peruse through the registry.

When Peter told him that he couldn't see it, Happy became furious with anger. He had not traveled so far to allow a minimum wage goat to stand between him and his arch nemesis. With a quick Google search he found Peter's address, went to his house, found his wife and kids, and delicately placed their heads, hands, and feet into a beautiful gift basket. Shortly after he returned to the help desk, and with an uncanny display of affection, offered the present.

Moved with emotion, Peter began to sob uncontrollably. Alas, as Happy's further requests to see the registry were denied with fitful, through inappropriate rage, Happy was forced to force feed him what was left of his family until the goat's stomach burst, leaving the help desk now unattended, and, far more importantly, leaving the registry unprotected.

TABLET: XXXVII

Happy stared at the registry, looking for his sworn enemy's room number, when the glass doors to The Hotel slammed open. They shattered upon impact and sent shards scattering everywhere.

A Black Wind blew into the lobby, and the stench of death was detected by Happy on the coattails of the wind. The air swirled about the room, tightening into a tornado in the middle of the lobby, where in a flash, it transformed into a being. The fell creature stood wearing a lavish black tuxedo garnished with the finest red and blue velvet. In each of his two hands he brandished a full sized maul. The maul in his left hand was forged of onyx, with ivory runes tattered across it. The maul in his right hand was forged of ivory, with runes trickled across it in black sharpie. His skin was a pale white, and he openly displayed his fangs, which could mean only one thing. He was a vampire.

The vampire spoke. "I am Ethnocentric Dracula."

Happy stared at the creature for some time, wondering what this meant to his cause. Fifteen minutes passed and not much had changed, so Happy spoke. "Dracula..." But Ethnocentric Dracula interrupted him.

"My name is Ethnocentric Dracula."

Happy began again. "Ethnocentric Dracula, why is it you are here? And why have you presented yourself to me?"

TABLET: XXXVIII

Before the foul, but well dressed, monster could respond to Happy Barrypants' inquiry, a dark figure crossed Happy's field of vision. "What the fuck is THAT thing?" Happy unwittingly blurted out. They both turned, for hovering in the air above the help desk was a pitch black orb the size of a bowling ball. It quivered with majesty, and shook with the weight of its ungodly power.

Ethnocentric Dracula, though filled with a dread only the undead could comprehend, knelt, and lowered his head to the thing. Happy stared blankly, dumbfounded, as the entity opened its nearly twenty eyes and stared...

"Do I smell French Fries?" Happy muttered inquisitively under his breath.

"BARRY HAPPYPANTS!!! I am the Elusive Black Potato! KNOW that in the future, my power will course within your family's veins. Soon, the race of Green Pig Men will be no more, and you and your family and friends will be its only survivors. You must venture to the planet of Porkucopia, for there lies the secret of the mark on your left testicle, and how it will aid you in harnessing my powers. The greatest secret of all, I will tell you now. The fate of the Universe lies in the hands of the legendary warrior... And his name is–"

The Elusive Black Potato was cut short when an explosion rocked the side of The Hotel's grandiose lobby.

"Ethnocentric Dracula! Your time has come!" The voice reverberated with pure evil, and everyone froze in terror.

Ethnocentric Dracula slowly raised his head, and spoke the words he had wished he'd never utter again. "Multinational Mummyman..."

TABLET: XXXIX

The Mummyman stepped over the rubble and through the hole blown in The Hotel's side. He was enormous: more than seven feet tall, and wrapped from head to toe in brightly colored maps, such that only his burning red eyes could be seen. Ethnocentric Dracula did not hesitate. He made his two mighty mauls mash Multinational Mummyman's melon, but to no avail. The Mummy laughed an unspeakably evil laugh. "You can no longer harm me, for I have the power of Rand McNally on my side!!" E. Dracula vomited blood in sheer terror.

Suddenly, whoosh! The Mummy was cut in twain, and Happy stood in repose, his sword dripping ichor. E. Dracula fell to Happy's feet, and kissed them. "For saving me from the unspeakable evil of Multinational Mummyman, I shall accompany you on your quest, oh mighty one." Realizing that all great heroes have a sidekick, Happy accepted E. Dracula's offer, on one condition...

TABLET: XL

Happy knew that Ethnocentric Dracula was a beast of the night, one who thirsted for blood and the essence of the living. Happy understood this, for he in fact thirsted for much of the same (well, he didn't LIVE off the essence of the living, but it sure gave him one hell of a good buzz). Happy allowed E. Dracula to travel with him so long as the carnage of the dark beast did not at any time exceed his own. Ethnocentric Dracula agreed, and soon both were well on their way havoc donned vengeance.

It should be noted that while E. Dracula realized that traveling with Happy would afford him many opportunities to slay those not like him, he on some level recognized that Happy too was not one of his own. This would haunt the plucky vampire later, but for now he ignored this fact in light of the vast sea of non-vampires there were left to slay.

The two set out into The Hotel; forgetting that they could use the registry to find Gribulor, and began to rampage through The Hotel floors. It was difficult to say who laid out a more furious visage of destruction. Each was fueled by their own personal hatreds. In the end, the two met at the doors of the High Lord's Suite, where Gribulor was undoubtedly residing. Happy spoke unto E. Dracula, "Do me the honors of a grand entrance, but forget not our agreement."

E. Dracula replied, "Indeed!" and annihilated the doors with his glorious mauls. Scantily clad women scattered from the entrance way, and the pair made short work of Gribulor's playthings. Soaked in blood and picking the trifling entrails of 27 concubine goats from their clothes, the duo found no evidence of Gribulor, dead or alive on the premises. Amidst the sea of death, E. Dracula noticed something peculiar in the far bedroom. There, under the back leg of the dresser in the closet, was a poker chip used to level it.

"A clue!" proclaimed E. Dracula.

"They must be at the Carnie Casino," retorted Happy, "a Casino revered around the Universe for its carnie game-and-ride atmosphere. Gribulor must be there!" And at that they were off.

TABLET: XLI

"I'll meet you out front!" E. Dracula exclaimed, and leapt through the window.

Happy trotted through the blood and carnage of the slaughter, and took the elevator down (putting it on an emergency stop for several minutes as he cleaned himself). As the door clicked open to The Hotel lobby,

Happy was outraged! The Elusive Black Potato had vanished, and far worse, the split body of Multinational Mummyman was gone, and in its place all that was left was a burned outline of his corpse's outline, and a map of Blahtvia.

Happy burst into the lobby, and lifted one of the dazed bell-goats in the air by his beard. "What happened to the masked mapped man!?"

"I.. I don't know. I just got here from the upstairs," he bleated. "All I know... is that on my way down I was passed by a hoard of security agents. I overheard them say the High Lord's suite was assaulted by a Scorpion-chicken and a well-dressed duck... Just like you folks."

Happy was even more outraged at the uselessness of the information. "You're coming with us!" he shouted, and he knocked the Goat unconscious by butting heads. He tossed his hostage over his shoulder, and ran out into the street in a panic. Nearly twenty empty police vans filled the avenue. *Where's that damned vampire?* he thought, as a massive crimson tank with flesh colored treads suddenly bashed through the unmanned blockade. The license plate on the front said Blood O'maticator, and he knew that it was his ride. Happy climbed up to the top of the tank, and hopped in.

"Who's the goat?" E. Dracula asked, as he flipped the tank into overdrive, and aimed it at the third moon (where the Carnie Casino was located).

"He's our ticket into the Casino. It's a surefire bet that Gribulor'll think a Green Pig is after him for vengeance over Barry Happypants' death."

"Barry Happypants, that's the name the Elusive Black Potato mentioned... But it still doesn't answer my question Happy."

"Let's just say I need a disguise... and there's nothing more effective than a *goatee*."

The tank lurched into the air, and they were off.

TABLET: XLII

They soon arrived at the Casino, and upon paying the fee of $8.75, parked the tank. By this time, it had dawned on Happy that he no longer bore his true form. Since the average lay-goat described him a scorpion-chicken, he realized he'd never be mistaken for a Green Pig again. With great sadness he tossed the skinned goat into the back seat, and bid farewell to the goatee adventures he'd been daydreaming of on his voyage. *Perhaps, one day...* Happy wiped a tear from his eye. "Lets go," he managed to say.

Happy and E. Dracula entered the Casino, where they were immediately assaulted by the glowing, multicolored neon lights, the sounds of clinking slot machines, and the mechanical roar of the Universe's largest indoor roller coaster. Little did the owners of the Carnie Casino know, that the Colon Casino, only three moons over, was building an indoor roller coaster of their own to dwarf theirs, but the less said about such matters the better.

They quickly decided to split up, and confidently went their separate ways, each determined to find Gribulor first. But when E. Dracula returned to their designated rendezvous point an hour later, he found Happy seated at the blackjack table, roaring drunk, and with his hand down some showgirl's top. "I assume you found nothing." E. Dracula sighed.

"I found this table," Happy exclaimed, "where

get this they serve you free booze and let you bet with chips instead of money!!" He fell to the ground in a fit of hysterics.

Having overheard him, the casino manager stepped forward. "I'm afraid, sir," he said from underneath a pencil-thin mustache, "that the chips are merely representative of money. You owe us three thousand dollars."

"But I don't have three thousand dollars!" Happy announced.

"Very well then, sir, perhaps you can work off your debt by washing our dishes." It was now Happy's turn to sigh. He cautiously reached for his sword. *Curses! Will my endless task of blood-soaked rampage and carnage ever truly end?*

TABLET: XLIII

Happy could not come up with a solution. The world whirled about him as he struggled for an answer. Then, in a flash of inspiration that could only come to one in Happy's drunken state, he knew what he had to do. Happy looked to E. Dracula, whose eyes had started to water at the notion of being bound to manual labor, subduing his mission of race-segregated carnage through the Universe and nodded. Unspoken, each knew what the other was thinking. Or so they thought.

E. Dracula drew his fierce mauls, ready for combat, only to find that Happy had drawn his zippo lighter, lit it, threw it on the table, raised his hands in the air, and started singing the lyrics to, "We Didn't Start the Fire."

E. Dracula could do nothing but watch, and he also knew that this could mean only one thing... Happy had also trained under Grand-Master Le Ok' Nknurk, the last French Master of Black Chu (the long lost French style of martial arts). When E. Dracula realized this, he made gesture for the two to combine in a two-person technique that would hopefully devastate the opposition.

E. Dracula lit a cigarette and started wantonly yet articulately criticizing the tacky carnie surroundings; "The embouchure of that ball tossing booth is clearly reminiscent of carnivals not of any time period represented here! Ah Ah Ah!" In the sheer moment of dumbfoundedness that overtook the carnies working the casino, Happy annihilated the inner essence of anyone within earshot of the remark. The circus of murder and destruction that ensued rivals that of the carnie tales of ancient twisters that would obliterate entire carnivals leaving only piles upon piles (or as the common folk say, "big piles") of carnie carnage.

As the two walked away from the smoldering wreckage of the once proud casino, all that could be said was that the stench of burnt blood-soaked cabbage lingered over the entire moon and onwards throughout the rest of the galaxy.

TABLET: XLIV

While the Dynamic Duo of Demolition and Destruction dashed away from the smoldering casino in search of their tank amidst the fleeing carnies, something far more dangerous lurked hundreds of kilometers beneath their feet.

Deep within the foul chambers of the Midget Galactic Headquarters located within the bowels of the

Carnie's Moon, the Maniacal Midget Mastermind Rupert the Conqueror was scheming a scheme most dastardly. He shuffled his miniature feet as he paced across the super-miniaturized landscape of the Goat Home Planet's Capital City. "Vat ve should have been doing vas to activate ze vinal vasc of ze plan to conquer ze Vorld. But instead it has come to my attention zat var above us ze vamous Larry BappyMaps, my Higlorian arch-nemesis, has returned yet again to haunt my dreams of conquering ze vorld!!!"

The Very High Very Small Council shuddered with fright, as Rupert turned and waved his mini-ray-gun at the council angrily. "Tell me you vools! How can zis being be destroying our cover operation, if he is still in ze confinement chamber!?" Rupert the Conqueror tapped a hidden button on the mini-skyscraper next to him, and the model mountain of Hornywood Heights opened to reveal a large tube. It contained within it none other than the body of the comatose Higlorian God Larry BappyMaps! The Council members gasped and muttered amongst themselves.

"Quiet villains!" Rupert bellowed monstrously. "It must be a trick of Gribulor's design designed to lure out his enemies. Find zis Clone of Larry Bappymaps and obliterate him at all costs! Sleeper cells across ze galaxy must be avakened! Ancient tomes must be rezearched for another vay of defeating our ageless opponent! Higlorians the Universe over must be punished and tortured for ze true secret of disposing their God vonce more. And most of all, Gribulor must pay for doing something so sinister as to resurrect through advanced genetic engineering ze enemy of midgets everywhere. But first, ze super zecret weapon designed to conquer ze vorld vill be activated!!! Oh, and ze duck too vill pay."

Amidst roars of approval, Rupert the Conqueror, turned and laughed endlessly as the mega-machine disguised as a roller-coaster which nearly spanned 1000 km within the moon, activated. "Hahaha! Villainy! Vonderful Villainous Villainy!"

Meanwhile, our heroes above were still unable to find the tank. "Not a tank. Not a tank. Not a tank..." E. Dracula quipped as he mashed and mangled each passing car to make finding his tank logically easier.

Happy's keen Higlorian whiskers perked up. "Do you hear that strange whine E.D.? I swear it sounds like..."

TABLET: XLV

But before he could finish, the ground opened up beneath them, and from its depths shot what appeared to be - no indeed it was! - a roller coaster track. The whine grew louder, and soon upon the track could be seen a missile moving at tremendous speed. "Look out!" E. Dracula shouted, but it was too late. The missile hit Happy squarely in the chest, and carried him careening into the sky.

What a predicament! Happy managed to think as he took his last atmospheric breath. The missile was hurtling through space, away from the moon and towards the planet of the Great Goat-Men. Happy struggled against the enormous g-force exerted on him by the missile's speed in an effort to reach the missile's control panel, but to no avail.

Meanwhile, one starship floating above the planet was paying careful attention to the hurtling missile, for inside that spaceship was none other than

Gribulor, feared ruler of the Great Goat-Men, who had escaped Carnie Casino during the chaos!

"So," Gribulor said to himself, for he was in the habit of speaking aloud to no one in particular. "I recognize those markings! The symbol of Rupert the Conqueror. Takulor!" Gribulor shouted to his pilot. "Use the arms to grab that projectile." Two large mechanical arms emerged from the vessel's belly, and caught the missile in mid-flight. With the sudden lurching halt of the missile, Happy only just barely managed to keep his grip, which was altogether preferable to floating helplessly in space for the rest of his existence.

The missile and its passenger were brought aboard, and Gribulor seemed pleased. "A Higlorian, and a brave one at that!" he said. "Tell me young one, what are you called?"

Happy couldn't believe his luck. Here was his sworn enemy, unaware and unsuspecting, and who could be felled if Happy just waited for the right moment. "My name," he whispered, "is..."

TABLET: XLVI

At that moment the ship jolted violently. Gribulor commanded his crew. "On screen; damage report." Outside was the crimson tank of Ethnocentric Dracula.

In realizing who had just attacked the ship; Happy spoke out, "Ethnocentric Dracula."

Gribulor took this to be his name, and replied, "Well, I suppose you can't change what your parents name you."

Inside the Blood O' maticator, the musings of

Gangsta Rap artist Master P's masterpiece, "Make them say Uhhh," (let the pages of time show that Ethnocentric Dracula was a Nubian) blared as the Vampire, shuddering with hatred, spoke softly to himself. "They're all different, they all must pay".

With a volley from the tank's primary cannon, a hole was torn in Gribulor's ship. Crew members began cascading into space from the crippled Daemon Ways.

Gribulor bellowed out a Goat-Man war cry. "WE'LL SETTLE THIS LIKE THE GO-O-O-ATS WE AR-R-R-RE!!!!"

TABLET: XLVII

As our hero was about to wield his scorpion tail and strike at the heart of his fearsome enemy, he was lifted up by the pull of the vacuum of space, and flew helplessly towards the hole in the ship. Gribulor, who wore magnetic boots at all times, was unaffected by the disturbance and moved towards his control panel. "I'll save you, Ethnocentric Dracula, and defeat our common enemy Rupert!" Gribulor jammed on the emergency shield generator, and the hole was instantly sealed. With a thud, our hero fell to the ground. "Takulor! Respond with a counterattack of tin cans!"

But a second volley of missiles smashed against the bridge of Gribulor's Command Ship the Daemon Ways. The barrage knocked out its sensors, and in a horrible explosion, instantly killed everyone on the main deck but Gribulor and our hero. Happy stood and rushed back into the bridge, unsheathing his sword as he entered. "Dracula! Arm that battle station or we'll surely be slain! Too late!!!" A third volley of projectiles appeared on the view-panel, but this time they were not from the tank! They smashed into the Blood O'maticator, as well as the Daemon Ways bridge. "They're being launched from the 3rd moon!" Gribulor screamed in outrage and shock.

Hundreds of metallic objects started drilling their way into the hull of each ship. The crimson tank lurched under the strain of the assault, and floated helplessly away in space as Ethnocentric Dracula was no doubt engaged in a fearsome struggle of his own... But here on the bridge, Gribulor pulled out his Demon Sword and readied himself for combat. "Dracula! To arms! The enemy has arrived!"

Confused, and utterly bewildered at the strange twist of fate, Happy was forced to fight side by side with his sworn enemy as a wave of midget attack droids entered through shields which only protected from the vacuum of space, and began pouring into the ship. Seconds seemed like minutes, which in turn seemed like hours, as the two powerful warriors battled the endless hoard of robotic monstrosities that bleeped and blooped in murderous rage. Nearly ten times in the ensuing combat, Happy was forced to fend off metallic claws instead of striking sweetly at Gribulor's defenseless back. Finally, as the bridge was cleared of its invaders, Gribulor and Happy turned to each other, swords and bodies covered in blood and oil. Gribulor lowered his head and grinned evilly. Before words could be exchanged, Happy, for he was facing the view screen, screamed, "Look out!!!"

Gribulor looked and bleated in outrage as missile launched from the badly damaged Blood O'maticator and smashed into the bridge. Happy dove and knocked Gribulor aside as the explosion wracked the bridge. In the seconds that followed, Gribulor saved both of their lives by switching on the emergency escape pod located directly beneath his command chair. Moments later Gribulor and Happy were sitting next to each other in a cramped pod that was careening towards the third moon.

"You saved my life!" they each said to each other... But through the view-panel they could see an endless barrage of missiles passing them by, launched from hundreds of roller coaster tracks that surfaced on the craters of the Midget Mastermind's Moon.

TABLET: XLVIII

Ethnocentric Dracula watched as waves of interplanetary missiles rocketed towards the escape pod. During this moment of pregnant pause, the Elusive Black Potato floated out from his back pocket (for it had made its way there at some point during the hubbub of the past few hours, do not dare question the mad skillz of the E.B.P.), and it spoke in its queer abhorrent tones.

"Happy is on that escape pod! You must rescue him and proceed on your quest!"

"Great Gribulor's Ghost!" E. Dracula exclaimed. He launched the tractor beam, ensnared the pod, and quickly brought it on board his damaged, but still functional, tank. When he opened the hatch, he was shocked to find Gribulor and Happy holding hands.

"Ethnocentric Dracula!" Happy blurted out.

"How extraordinary..." Gribulor whispered discretely. "These two beings have the same name..."

But E. Dracula had already drawn his mauls. "Taste death, Goat tyrant!" he cried, and swung his weapons at Gribulor. But Gribulor, trained in the ancient, deadly art of ducking, ducked, and E.D.'s mauls smashed into one another, shattering them both to a hundred pieces, each.

"Wait!" Happy cried. "He doesn't know who I am! We can use him to our own ends, that is, of course, until the moment comes... when we can take him completely by surprise and destroy him unawares!" E. Dracula and Gribulor both sighed, and by their quite different facial expressions, Happy realized he had spoken his words aloud, instead of whispering them softly and sweetly into the ear of his ally.

TABLET: XLIX

The three all stood there, each with the knowledge that none of them were in particularly good positions to trust one another. It seemed as if each had some innate desire to strike down one, or all, of their adversaries. And yet, each realized that making a move would leave them open, and prone to be eradicated by one of the others. This strange standoff would have gone on for hours, if not for the fact that the tank was still overrun by the relentless midget robot army. E. Dracula had merely tolerated them all this time, robots that they were.

Happy ended the stalemate by stating, "I think it's time to make an exit."

Ethnocentric Dracula laughed. "When we meet again, you gonna think you be fightin' TEN niggas. Ah, Ah, Ah!" and from there, turned around, snapped his fingers, and left. The chips of his maul evaporated at the sound. Gribulor simply walked off. All three went their separate ways, made independent use of their own one-time use disposable escape pods, and jetted off towards the third moon in formation.

Ethnocentric Dracula landed closest to the carnie base entrance. The recent events weighed least on his mind, for he sought only to eradicate those who were not his own. He waddled off towards the base, hungry for death.

Happy could see E.D. and the base on the horizon. He knew his only hope of leaving that God forsaken carnie infested cabbage pit lay within that base, and he soon began his journey. By the time Happy crested the hill near the carnie entrance, he found only a raging inferno instead.

TABLET: L

The night sky above him shone with a crimson hue, and the many moons of the nameless (within the confines of this Epic), Goat home-world gleaming in the massive background. Happy looked past the fires, which raged before him over five thousand feet into the air, and beyond the many moons, towards the home-world, around which a fleet of ships had apparently entered orbit from the atmosphere. It appeared the home-world was ensuing a massive exodus! Tens of thousands of ships cluttered the space-ways in a great goat traffic jam. Happy's gaze shifted now, to the moon 3 moons over, that housed the Colon Casino. "Great Gribulor's Ghost! It's changing!"

The moon had begun drifting towards the home-world, and as it did so, its surface shook with such vibration that its outer shell exploded outward, and revealed a massive missile! Apparently, the world's soon-to-be largest indoor roller coaster was merely the inner workings of an Epic doomsday device which was currently being unleashed at the home planet of his arch nemesis! Egads! The Colon Casino was forever known as the primary opposing enterprise to Rupert the Conqueror's Casino, which was truly just a front for Rupert's mischievous midget empire. And here it was that Rupert's fake competition, had really been a well-orchestrated and impossible to reveal cover all along! Rupert even owned the competition!

"Ahh the irony, the wondrous irony. Hahahahaha! HAHAHA!" Happy bellowed maniacally, as the missile hurtled towards Gribulor's planet. "The end of your entire world is nigh, Gribulor! And I will be here to watch it burn!!!!"

But as Happy's insidious laughter filled the night sky as vibrantly as the burning casino, Gribulor the Great, who had snuck up behind Happy while he was witnessing the spectacle, raised his Demon Sword upon high, and upon speaking his ancient curse, "Die, you fucking fuck!" chopped off Happy's head once again...

And now it was dark, too dark for the corporate special assassin to see from the position he was crouched in.

TABLET: LI

Far below him, the shadowy figures moved quietly in the darkness, their dark robes rustling in the night. He leapt down, silently, and slew the five figures with a series of quick, deadly, accurate blows. But without warning he found himself weak, and the darkness all around him seemed to grow. He swooned, and was unconscious before he hit the ground... Soon, the darkness cleared, and a bright white light blinded him. But when he reached to rub his eyes, horror overtook him. There were no limbs to answer his brain's command!

Happy was back in the jar of fluid as a bodiless head lingering on far beyond its natural time. The room was awash with rows of lights, and other heads in jars were placed evenly around the room. Large ornate doors opened to the side, and in poured schoolchildren and their teachers. His eyes raised in disbelief, Happy saw finally where he was: "Hall of Defeated Enemies: Gribulor National Museum of Triumph."

TABLET: LII

It was Mary-Marie-Jane's eighth birthday. She wanted a bio-pony ever so much, just like all the other human metamorph's had. But her father was an important bio-engineer, and instead preferred for her to attend the very expensive, and very elite, school of bio-medics, where no ponies were allowed under any circumstances.

No. This was her birthday, and instead of riding the ponies in a beautiful swamp, she was forced to learn with her class, about all those stupid ancient brains, you know, the ones that were eternally tortured by being forced to relive their demise at the hands of their arch-nemesis forever. Every time they succeeded in killing Gribulor, the program would just reset, and their memories were erased! You know, so they didn't know they were doing it all over again.

How boring! She instead fantasized about wandering the Great Hoofed Rock Terrace, or the Magnificent Watery Drinking Hole... When she was suddenly distracted, from even her daydreams! She allowed her classmates to follow ahead, while she looked bewildered at one of the brains.

Instead of being in its state of endless blissful slumber, it was looking directly at her, and was... winking? She walked up close to the tube, pressed her face against the glass, and smiled down upon it the cute little thing. "Hello there little thing... What's your name?" she cooed, as she tapped the bio-chamber and made eyes at Happy.

Suddenly, without warning, and to her surprise, the eyes shot out and exploded against the glass! The tube shattered and unleashed a flood of sticky yellow containment goo, also in the process blowing Mary-Marie-Jane's face off. The brain initiated its jet-pack procedures, entered her head, forced her old brain out, and activated its cloak subroutine, creating a makeshift turban out of anything in the area. Since the only thing to use was her dress, he ripped it off, revealing her poke-pony underwear, and wrapped his skull in it.

"Miss Mary-Marie-Jane, what have you done?!" the teacher barked, as her and all the stunned classmates ran up to the broken chamber.

TABLET: LIII

"Nothing," a strangely deep voice issued from her mouth. "Now come over here where no one can see, so I can show you what I found."

The other children and the teacher foolishly fell for the ruse, and when the little girl unwrapped the skull, a laser flash issued from its eye-sockets, and all were instantly vaporized, leaving not so much as a thin layer of dust. The skull was wrapped again, and Mary-Marie-Jane left the museum. From there she traveled to the nearest intergalactic reconstitution chamber.

The man on duty peered at the strange girl before him. "What can I do for you?" he asked.

She looked back and forth, and when she was sure no one was looking, showed him the skull. Whoosh! A powerful wind sent him hurtling up into the air, and far, far into the distance.

TABLET: LIV

Happy's corporate training not only afforded her easy access to the reconstitution chambers, but also gave her the very knowledge necessary to operate the devices therein. Inside the core lab (where all the "magic" takes place), the ever resourceful Happy activated the reconstitution chamber, started infusing the Keg-O-Stem-Cells, and hopped in for what she had hoped would be a most elegant and exact rebuilding of the Happy that was green, pig, and male. Unfortunately, because anyone that could run the lab was left dead by Happy's well-honed espionage skills, she could all but watch as her transmogrification was imbued with the entire Keg-O-Stem-Cells; far too much for any being in creation. The process which followed redefined the limits of horror from that day on.

Happy, for a moment, enjoyed his supple green skin... only to watch as a bony carapace enveloped all of his body. Internal organs began to grow around this exo-endoskeleton. Happy tried to scream in terror, but he was in a state of flux, and all breath had left him.

Around his exo-internal organs, the body of Mary-Marie-Jane grew again, only larger... much, much larger. So large in fact that the body at about the height of 12 feet could no longer occupy any reconstitution chamber in the known Universe. The partially formed (and thus hideous), 12 foot, 700 pound monster groaned as it rolled from the shards of the broken chamber to the floor.

Happy was helpless to do anything inside this abominable living cocoon, though he was at least aware of sounds and motions.

From inside the monster, Happy heard goats yell, "Stop! Museum Police! Come out with your.... OH MY GOD!!!!! Render that thing unconscious men!"

TABLET: LV

Happy struggled helplessly as he wiggled his brain back and forth, but it was all to no avail. "Nooo!!!! The horrible lasery carnage! Fall back!!! Its beginning to mutate!!" The cries of the merciless slaughter were like music to him though, and soothed the agony of his inability to see or feel what was taking place around him. Happy's form occasionally shook uncontrollably, for the reconstitution chamber had been unable to complete the hideous transformation. This would never have happened if it didn't beak, as they were never designed large enough, thanks to the inventor Dr. Allaways Bentover, the known midget supporter. His oversight had left our giant hero in a state of quantum instability!

With sounds like popping corn, the massive creature transmogrified into 27 identical Barry Happypants clones! Upon reaching consciousness, they all rose to their feet, and stared at each other. All were verily bewildered to the point of paralysis. The original form (since it contained the real brain), was unaffected by the bewildering bewilderment, and took several steps backwards and away from his clones, only to trip over something that was right behind him!

"Stupid Goddamned uneven floor!" he cried, before noticing he'd stumbled over some strange metallic thing, of many legs, caged in solid emerald. It spoke to his subconscious with gravity waves, and as Happy confirmed that it was not a paradox, that this creature of solid silver and alloyed mercury belonged in his Universe as naturally as dust, the emerald cracked and vanished. Once within this reality, whole, free, it crawled up his face, and built a web of manufactured silicon and borrowed carbon between his ears, where it climbed into and replaced his left pupil.

It stared out into the world, both with a renewed sense of vengeance, and a ferocity unseen for generations.

"Quick! Before they start snapping out of it! Get your hands on a weapon, and soon!"

Happy, stumbled to his feet. "What the fuck? Did my eye just say something?"

"Yes, moron, in there quick!" And from his eye issued forth a laser beacon that spelled out, "In Here Stupid," on the door next to him, which was coincidentally marked, "Ancestral Weapons and Cafeteria."

Happy, burst in through the door, and several moments later, burst out from the door, only this time brandishing an Ancestral Shotgun, an Ancestral Ammo Bandolier, and 12 Ancestral Burritos.

"Come and get it, Pig Scum! It's wiener schnitzel time!" he issued forth... into the empty room...

TABLET: LVI

"Great Gribulor's Ghost!" he cried. "They've all become invisible!"

And he was soon proven right, for he was nigh but instantly pummeled by the many invisible clones, who each in their turn said, "Take that!"

With no alternative, Happy fired his Ancestral Shotgun randomly into the room. Invisible blood splattered everywhere. When his ample supply ammo was finally spent, Happy grasped the nearest invisible clone and tore him apart with his bare hands. By now invisible blood covered Happy from head to toe. But at last, at long last, Happy was the last Happy standing.

"Phew!" he moaned with exhaustion. "I'm thirsty! I'll drink some of this water on the floor." Happy drank deeply of the clear liquid, unaware it was the blood of his clones. "Ugh," he gargled. "Tummy no feel too good."

TABLET: LVII

Happy keeled over and puked like a college freshman who'd been out drinking all night. The primordial Happy ooze within the invisible blood combined with the 3 Ancestral Burritos Happy had eaten previous to exiting the cafeteria. All mixed in his stomach to form the Ancestral Happy Burrito Monster.

Off in the distance, the bass line of the song, "Milkshake," could be heard getting louder and louder as if whatever played the music was approaching. A moment later the Blood O'maticator burst through the lab wall, blasting the popular tune as much as it blasted the concrete apart. From the bowels of the tank leapt the insidious Ethnocentric Dracula, along with his two vampire-fowl cohorts, Midas and, 'L'.

Simultaneous to the arrival of the vampires, Multinational Mummyman crashed through the ceiling. Forty of Gribulor's S.W.A.T. members also happened to arrive at the scene right about then. By means which cannot be explained to this day, Miss Mary-Marie-Jane's zombie rose from the offal of the 27 Happy clones. Lastly, arriving fashionably late (in this case a few seconds), by special mental teleportation, was Rupert the Conqueror holding hands with Grand Master Le Ok' Nknurk, the last French Master of Black Chu.

Happy clung to his Ancestral Shotgun, and with a slight twitch in his green neck, loaded it with the last few shells that remained to him.

TABLET: LVIII

Ethnocentric Dracula raised his wings, and flapping them upon high pronounced, "Them that's different, gotta pay the piper!" His sidekicks, Midas and 'L', pronounced merely the special fx of arming themselves with rocket propelled grenade launchers, and regular grenade launchers, respectively.

From far above, as he brandished his signature throwing star / double-barrel shotgun super-weapon, the voice of Clito Von Herschiza, the super-elite lieutenant that commanded a crack commando squad, sounded, "Red Team go Ducks! Blue team go Pigs! And I'll go for the–"

Clito's rope snapped, and he fell right into Multinational Mummyman's arms. Rupert the Conqueror roared with laughter, for he was about to have his sweet sweet vengeance against Ethnocentric

Dracula for his costly assault that ruined quite an expensive casino.

As the Grand Master lit a cigarette and back-flipped across the room, and while Miss Mary-Marie-Jane moon-walked towards the leftover clone brains, our hero became overcome by a massive pain in his eye. What had begun as a minor tonal hum, similar to being a brain in a jar, became a harmonic vibration that seemed like it was going to rip his entire body apart from the inside out. Happy clutched at his head, as if he wanted to rip his skull apart. "What's happening to MEEEE??!?"

The vibration stopped as sudden as it had begun, and everything fell into an eerie silence. Everything, and everyone in the room was completely still. They were all frozen in space, and time. Happy tiptoed across the room, examining the fight scene, when a voice rang out in the air.

"I've slowed down time to give you a more effective combat scenario. Consume your fill of blood-thirst and then let's be on our way, shall we?" his eye chimed.

Happy shrugged. It didn't seem like that bad of an idea, no matter who, or what, it came from. And besides, if it was *his* eye, he might as well trust it. He crept across the room towards Multinational Mummyman, who Happy had once before slain, and had missed the opportunity to steal some maps... when suddenly, the Elusive Black Potato exploded in its fried fiery glory into the center of the room.

It hovered in mid air, and began to speak, when suddenly again the Drunken Wanderer fell from the sky, and landed in a drunken stupor at Happy's boot-heel. THEN out of nowhere, the tiny man garbed in green, from much earlier, you remember him right, appeared before them all in a puff of cannabis smoke.

They spoke all together, and in unison... "You are our only hope, many-named warrior. You must go to... (Porkucopia! Whiskey Mountain! The Land of Og!) and you must rescue (The Blood Monkey Prophet! The last magic jug of whiskey! The ever smoking pipe!) and only then will I help you." Happy cocked his shotgun, and took two steps back.

TABLET: LIX

"What is this never-ending madness??? Shall it never cease??" Happy cried out in confusion and anger. He began haphazardly firing his Ancestral Shotgun around the room. BOOM! Multinational Mummyman exploded in a puff of maps. BOOM! The zombie of Mary-Marie-Jane was splattered against the wall. BOOM! The bloody head of the Drunken Wanderer flew across the room. BOOM! Midas doubled over, his chest pouring blood from the gaping hole therein. CLICK! The Ancestral Shotgun was out of ammo, and Happy felt his nervous twitch worsen.

"Mwahahahaha!" An evil laugh filled the room, emanating from the gem in Happy's eye.

"ENOUGH!" the Elusive Black Potato boomed, and a great light and energy filled the room, and everything became frozen. "Hippy Dippy Zippy Do!" the Black Potato intoned.

Happy felt a great pain in his eye as the gem was ripped from his socket and floated up into the air, where it confronted the equally levitating Elusive Black Potato.

"We meet again," the gem said.

"And for the last time, Shockingly Evil Gemstone of Sung-Sing Road!" the Black Potato replied. And with that, the Potato and Gemstone entered into an immortal combat, which cannot be described in words. The battle grew so fierce that the very limits of time and space began to be ripped asunder.

Happy felt his body contort and twist as a gaping black hole appeared beside him. It started sucking up his enemies and friends like a vacuum, for indeed it was a vacuum, that is the very definition of the effect of a black hole after all, at least according to popular myth anyway.

Happy reached out to grasp something, anything, but his outstretched fingers failed to find a hold, and into the black hole he was swept.

TABLET: LX

It was dark, too dark for the corporate special assassin to see from the position he was crouched in. 35, 34, 33, the seconds ticked away until he was supposed to spring on his mark. The seconds seemed like months as they rattled in the silent killer's head. He jumped up into classic battle-stance, brandished his Ancestral Shotgun, and promptly, and violently, vomited the four uneaten Ancestral Burritos (which he'd pocketed), in sheer terror. Everything seemed so familiar... But this time... He remembered everything!

Looming like a mountain in the purple illuminated void above him was a monstrous orb, with more eyes and hideous foaming many-teethed tentacle mouths than stars in the sky. Scattered about him were the bloodied battle-torn remains of everything and everyone from the before, except for... Ethnocentric

Dracula and Rupert the Conqueror, who were unwittingly holding hands thinking each to be their sidekicks, and 'L' and Grandmaster Le Uk'Nkurk, who were also holding hands several feet over, only they knew what was going on, and were simply comforting one another.

The Elusive Black Potato and the Shockingly Evil Gemstone Eye, ceased their hovering fury, and turned to address the enormous many-teethed deity in whose monstrous presence they all now resided.

"You... are in violation... of... my... sanctuary! Puny orbs... of pitiful... miniature... midget size! Feel my... wrath... if... you do not... adequately explain... this disturbance!" All Universes and all realities resounded with this William Shatner like commandment.

The Elusive Black Potato started to speak, but the Shockingly Evil Gemstone flew forth into the sky at tremendous speeds, and spoke first. "Oh great and powerful Grand Onion! Forgive our pathetic intrusion into your realm, but we come to seek sanctuary here! My master and I are being hounded by the Elusive Black Potato and his wacky band of fowl cohorts. Kill them all, and in return, we will give you their souls."

Far below, Happy scratched his head. He wasn't really sure if he should feel bad about turning Ethnocentric Dracula in for his own green hide, or cheer his eye on for the brilliant ruse.

The Elusive Black Potato protested. "Hear us, oh great and powerful Grand Onion! The orb of Sung-Sing is a fearsome fiend who flees and fabricates fairy-tales to fuel his fancy, and fool his foes! Free us, and forgive us! Return us to our land, and leave that orb to your own devices."

TABLET: LXI

The Grand Onion peered at Sung-Sing, then gave The Elusive Black Potato an equally hideous look. At long last the Grand Onion gave its reply. "It seems... that you're both wasting your breath with your petty bickering! Ain't nobody, not even ME, master of the Universes, got time for that! As punishment for this, you shall be forced to occupy the same body for as long as you both shall be!"

And at that, the Grand Onion winked with all of his eyes at once, and as Sung-Sing disappeared, the Elusive Black Potato grew. The Grand Onion spoke again. "And since I believe that this *all* has something to do with you, Barry Happypants, you shall be indentured with the care of this... thing... for the rest of your natural life, or whatever. Right where it belongs... in that empty eye socket of yours."

The Grand Onion stretched out one of his great tentacles and slapped the potato, such that it flew with such force into Happy's head that it should never be removed again. The Potato-Eye was truly monstrous to peer at. It looked as if Happy's eye had been overcome with some terrible cancer. When the deed was done, the Grand Onion spoke once more. "It seems that I need not punish anyone else. Go, and never return, else you shall face my wrath!"

Another portal opened, only it didn't suck as much, and all the combatants staggered towards the rift. Happy was last to go, but before he could step through the portal, the Grand Onion stopped the Green Pig and told him, "We expect great things from you."

TABLET: LXII

When Happy emerged again from the portal, he found himself on a barren plain. Far in the distance the setting sun bathed a great tower in a red glow. The Elusive Black Potato, although nearly powerless due to his transformation, was still able to speak to Happy in a telepathic whisper. "Go to the tower," he whispered sweetly to Happy, who dumbly obeyed.

By the time he reached the foot of the edifice it was nightfall. The tower was made of white marble, and now shone blue by the light of the twin moons. Happy made his way through the tiny gate, and ascended the 2,072 step spiral staircase that led to the top. What he found at the summit was more horrible than anything he could've conceived in even his most deranged imaginings, more terrible than what he could have dreamed in his worst fever dreams!!

He cried out, "Ahhhh!!!!! GAHHHH!!!!!" in pure unadulterated fear and surprise. There, upon a table in the center of the tower's roof, was his own head, severed and preserved in a jar of thick liquid.

It stared at him with two wide-open and unmutilated eyes!

What fate could the Gods possibly have in mind for Happy Barrypants!?

TABLET: LXIII

Our hero stumbled about in confused rage. His vision blurred, and madness started to overtake his fragile, though very violent, mind. In a telepathic whisper he heard, "The window. Go for the window." In his clouded state, he dumbly obeyed, and leapt through the open portal, defenestrating himself.

The wind picked up all around as he fell, and then, with a loud thud, everything faded into total black darkness...

And now it was dark, too dark for the corporate special assassin to see from the position he was crouched in. Our hero dropped onto the poor unsuspecting... Ethnocentric Draculas beneath him?

Happy landed in classic battle stance, and attacked with his truly specialized, double dead-cat maneuver?

As he spun with all his ferocious might, yet another portal opened up above him, and a strange orb hovered and glistened in the darkness. Overcome with desire to possess it as his precious, he jumped up with all his might, even going so far as to throw his cats down in an attempt to gain more velocity. But he missed it by several inches with his grasping hands... All he could read was the label on its side, "Orb of the Drunken Wanderer. Handle with care. Drink Frequently."

Beneath him, the Ethnocentric Draculas looked up, and prepared to tear Happy's body to shreds. And yet, just as as Happy fell into the midst of certain doom, he awoke at the base of the tower with a splitting headache.

"What the fuck?" he cried out in poetic verse.

TABLET: LXIV

Happy Barrypants exploded.

The End.

TABLET: LXV

* * * * * * * * * *

$$X = x + 1.$$
If $X = 999999$ goto Section X.
Goto Page 1.

* * * * * * * * * *

Section X:

It was dark. Droplets of water fell in an endless cacophony of bittersweet chaos. Vapors of rust and acetone filled the air with an acrid odor all too reminiscent of the deep forgotten underworld, the decaying remains of the original capital of the Goat Home-world Tincania. And it all resided beneath the foundation of their entire civilization. Of course it was here, in these lost depths, that the Eternal Time Capsule was kept.

Within its protective shell, the ETC safely encased four of the greatest heroes ever known to exist, in endless, timeless, eternal, satisfying, stasis.

In that final moment when the last living person left that section of the ancient city, that's when the drunken wanderer placed the Eternal Time Capsule there. And there it would remain undisturbed until such time that a need arose in the galaxy for a savior from somewhere, sometime, who resided in the mystery that makes the stuff legends are made from, which in turn are also mysterious.

Misty mysterious water filled the air, and with the sound of a stopping locomotive, the capsule doors opened. And lo and behold, groggily stepping up out of the titaniasteel doors, was Happy Barrypants, the legendary Green Pig hero, with his side kick Ethnocentric Dracula... And there as well was El Krunko, the Ultimate Legendary Green Pig Hero (although he, like his brother, was not actually green, nor a pig), with sidekick Miguel Sanchez Clone TK-421.

TABLET: LXVI

Heroes and sidekicks unite! The adventurers instantly recognized each other, and spent the next few hours getting to know one another as they shook off their time-sickness. Now that that's out of the way, the four mighty avengers ventured forth. But to where?

"I say we visit the Great Gold Wizard Abuhm-Ras," said TK-421. "Only he can restore my memories."

"That is a secondary task," El Krunko replied. "We must travel to the distant moon of Ger, where the most beautiful women in all the Universe can be found."

"No," said E. Dracula. "Gribulor the Great Goat-Man and Rupert the Conqueror must be vanquished."

"Indeed," intoned Happy. "But first, the Orb of the Drunken Wanderer must be recovered!"

The new-found friends were in a quandary. What possible solution could be offered that would not be reached by bloodshed? Happy's hand made its way towards the hilt of his sword. El Krunko licked his lips sinisterly.

"A coin!" offered TK-421. "Heads, I decide.

Tails, E. Dracula decides." The coin spun through the air.

TABLET: LXVII

"I decide!" The deep resonating voice hung heavy in the air, as Happy Barrypants drew his sword, and sliced the coin in twain.

El Krunko spoke aloud. "I demand that you show yourself, strange stranger!" The sidekicks stared in anticipatory amazement as Happy's monstrous eye spun violently in his head. A red laser beam emanated from the trembling orb, and etched a hologram figure upon the metal corridor wall. It created the red 8-bit form of a man on a camel, bearing red scimitars, and donned in a red cloak.

Though the eye produced the voice, the red holo-man moved his mouth and spoke. "My name is the Sing Potato, and I am the strongest warrior in the galaxy. In fact so strong, and so unstoppable, that I was forever cursed to be in two separate forms, one containing the sum of my evil, and the other the sum of my good. For thousands of years I traveled the world in split consciousness, ever attempting to conquer the other half of my nature... That is until this pig, Happy Barrypants, and his idiot band of cohorts somehow managed to stumble across the one deity who could restore me to my former self. A transformation he considered to be a curse, but was actually my saving grace. Though whole, I am forced to reside in his head as a Potato, until the final curse can be lifted, and I might roam the Universe again as more than just a hologram, in search of foes to destroy, lands to conquer, and conquests to be won."

Happy Barrypants shed tears from his other eye as he listened to the sad tale. Clearly annoyed, Ethnocentric Dracula crossed his wings and raised his beak, whereas El Krunko hoisted his Ancestral Chainsaw upon high and screamed at the top of his lungs. "Your quest is ours now! How might we assist?"

The hologram narrowed his beady red eyes, and muttered softly, as if the walls had ears. "To the Fortress of the Staircase. The boundary of Hell itself."

Miguel Sanchez Clone TK-421's eyes sparkled with desire and success.

His evil plan couldn't have been working out better.

TABLET: LXVIII

"Hell? Oh, I've been there before..." Happy explained. "And truly, the experience was hellish. But I know not how to return."

"I will direct you," the hologram Sing Potato replied. "From here, go south, through the under-dark of the civilizations above."

And so, they ventured southward, until they reached a small town. The unusually short denizens stared in wonder and amazement at the sight of the four wanderers. Before long they ended up at a local tavern. The innkeeper was astonished that he should have such strange beings as his guests, and he offered them their rooms for free, especially after watching the way in which Happy eyed his sword hungrily. Soon the four were drunk and rowdy. The hologram of Sing Potato, although long since returned to Happy's eye, felt left out of the revelry.

The evening passed in a blur. When Happy

awoke, a beautiful midget was combing her hair beside him. "You owe me 100 yardblats," she said.

"Foul succubus!" Happy swore, grabbed his sword, and beheaded her with one swipe.

The remaining three members of the band were awoken by the sound of banging on their doors. "Quickly!" they heard Happy shout. "The town is overrun with demons!"

The four rushed out into the street, and slew man, woman and child indiscriminately. They departed an hour later, the town burning behind them, no one left alive.

TABLET: LXIX

The four stood at the gates of Hell. El Krunko stepped forward. "I'll handle this!" he declared, as he gestured over to the sign right beside the gates of hell.

The sign read, "Abandon all hope, ye who enter here..." in a tasteful Gothic font. Below that it read, "...except El Krunko!" and that bit was written in blood. Happy and their sidekicks puzzled over what exactly that meant, but they all nodded in agreement because El Krunko thought it was cool. El Krunko further pointed out to his comrades that the blood was, in fact, the blood of, "The Beast."

El Krunko strut towards the gates, kicked them open with one kick of his boot, walked straight into Hell and yelled out, "I'M BACK BABY!"

Satan immediately appeared before the four of them (of which the other 3 were noticeably shaken, but still relatively heroic in embouchure), his one tentacle arm wrapped around a torturee, and his regular arm brandishing the barbed n' flaming whip he was using for said torture.

The Beast spoke in his surly Mexican voice. "Hola Gringos! Que pasa?"

"We have a problem, bitch!" El Krunko retorted as he spit at the feet of the Dark Lord.

TABLET: LXX

"No... There is no problem... There is only Zuul." The Dark Lord mumbled from his many tentacled mouth, which dribbled and oozed a nasty goo onto the floor. It smelt of sulfuric acid and burned teeny holes in the imported good-intentioned paving stones.

El Krunko's head tilted in disbelief, and as he came to realize the horrible truth, he began to fall back, astounded. "You... You're not Satan... You dropped that accent like you expected me to bend over! It.. It cannot be!" El Krunko stammered horrified.

"Are you... pigs?" it bellowed out monstrously, as it oozed even more goo upon the floor.

Before either of the Legendary Heroes could speak, Ethnocentric Dracula and Miguel Sanchez Clone TK-421 each piped in, "No."

The Satanic Imposter dribbled some more ooze and barked, "Then... ... ... Die!!!!", and as his mouth opened wide, many tentacled loogies lunged forth, and wrapped both sidekicks in instantaneous acidic death.

"Oh the horror! Kill me now for being unable to save them from this wrath!" Happy sobbed.

"Curse them non-pigs. Serves them right," El Krunko retorted.

The flesh sizzled and popped from their bodies, their bones melted, and Ethnocentric Dracula and Miguel Sanchez Clone TK-421, sidekicks to the Green

Pig heroes, were no more. However, since they were foul-mouthed, and foul-hearted, they instantly reappeared where they stood (for they were in Hell), however slightly paler.

Let it be known that from this day on, Ethnocentric Dracula was no longer a Nubian.

"Oh sugar," he quacked. "Peaches and cream."

The clone cursed to the air and shook his fist.

El Krunko reared up his Ancestral Chainsaw at seeing the monstrous changes bestowed upon his companions. "I'll avenge your disfigurement, noble followers! May your souls rest in Hell, Zuul." And reaching upon high, and swinging downward, El Krunko produced a striking blow upon the Dark Lord so swift and so well placed, that it sliced the Dark Lord in twain...

But all was not made well.

"You tool! You have only made me stronger this day. Fool! Zuul does not rest!" And thus forth, the Dark Lord became two dark lords, each identical, though half their original height. Happy Barrypants shivered and shook with fear, for he was not fond of acid (being a metal endoskeleton), and tentacles made him queasy.

El Krunko's eyes burned with a passion he had not felt since...

Since before the unknown amount of time he was trapped in the time capsule. Once again, reaching upon high and swinging downward, he sliced and repeated, diced and repeated, and slashed while repeating again and again. Like a chainsaw stuck on sputter by a spastic man who stutters, never before had so many attacks been made in one round of combat in history. Stone flew, tentacles poured, and acid rained... and as the sulphuric cloud settled, all that remained was

El Krunko... and fifty million pissed off mini-tentacle acidic dark lord beastlings.

"Quack this!" quacked Ethnocentric Dracula.

TABLET: LXXI

Happy, annoyed at this occurrence, and being a pig, decided to take manners into his own snout. Literally. Happy proceeded to eat all but one of the wee beasts. The last of Zuul squeaked, "You cannot defeat me so easily!!!" and he scurried off into the bowels of Hell.

El Krunko bellowed out (in typical El Krunko fashion), "Well then... Shall we?" And the group started off with Miguel Sanchez Clone TK-421 taking the lead.

"I've spent many a restless night down here with the big gringo," Miguel said. "And if anyone can find him, I can." So they descended into the circles of hell, only stopping to laugh at the souls submerged in molten sulfur, and the naked people with their heads turned backwards, wallowing in their own feces.

At long last they arrived in the ninth circle, where deep in the heart of the frozen wasteland they came across the true Dark Lord of the nether regions. Satan. There he sat, frozen and chewin' on some hardcore sinners. Satan hailed the four with his chin. "Ey Gringos! Long time, no see."

Miguel hailed back. "Yo ese! Que pasa?"

"Well, you know," Satan replied. "I gotta do some time down here in the frozen casa as usual meng. Need to keep up appearances... You know, for my peoples."

"Palabra!" retorted Miguel.

Happy decided to take the lead. "Sir, we have

been charged with a quest..."

"Si, Si." Satan interrupted. "I know what youz need, but I need something from y'all first. That's just how it is, esse. See, I got this little problem with a fellow y'all refer to as, 'God.' You just gotta take care of him for me meng. You know, like dispatch him for me. Knock him down son. You gotta put in that work, holmes. Comprende?"

TABLET: LXXII

The four adventurers paused in thought. Satan, thinking them to be planning out their method of attack on God, went about the business of toying with his food. An hour went by rather quickly. Happy leaned against some frozen sulfur to rest, while E.D. and Miguel Sanchez fell asleep on the ground. El Krunko stared off into space, scratching his chin, lost deep in his own meandering mind. Finally, after a long while, Ethnocentric Dracula sat up suddenly, and threw a glance at his partner. They nodded, each sensing what the other was thinking, and hailed Satan to look their way.

"Who?" they both chimed together.

Miguel Sanchez leapt to his feet and shouted proudly. "Forgive my compatriots, oh Dark Lord. I'll handle this one!" Satan merely nodded. "C'mon guys, I know what we have to do."

Without saying a word, the three shrugged, and followed Miguel back up the many layers of the Abyss, and out into the pale daylight of the upper world.

"What now, slave?" El Krunko whispered to his sidekick. "Tell me so I might lead us into the pages of history with our glorious glory-filled actions."

The clone of the great Miguel Sanchez pointed off into the far distance, beyond the underground Misty Mountains. Though he truly knew nothing about this God fellow Satan had spoken of, he desperately wanted to participate. Ever since he was reborn in hell he'd felt like he'd been a useless member of the adventure squad, in which he was playing only a minor role. His Epic plans for world conquest and the carefully wrought plans he'd laid out no longer seemed his cup of tea, and he was filled with ennui. But even so, his eyes radiated with the thrill of a grand adventure.

"To the land of the God's!" Miguel shouted. "I only hope that we might find it before we die of old age. Pennsylvania had mentioned something about God once to my original, and I'm pretty sure she was talking about a land on the Goat-Home world. I think it's in that direction. Maybe even above ground."

El Krunko and Happy agreed that it was better than nothing, and they set off on the journey.

The tales of their quest are lost to time, but know that it was filled with much carnage and merry-making as would be expected of them.

Eventually, they found themselves standing in the shadows of a megalithic signpost that marked the entrance to a chasm between the largest mountains in all the world. In standard tasteful Gothic font, it read, "Land of the Gigantic Oversized Dynamos this way. Land of Meaningless Annoying Neanderthals that way. Mortals not wanted. Bingo on Thursdays."

"This must be the place!" Happy explained. "But I'm not so sure we should go in... It says no mortals guys... Umm.... Guys?" Happy was talking to himself, for his allies had already ventured ahead.

After hours of uneventful walking, the band of

heroes came upon a massive entity. It loomed above them, nearly 500 feet in height, and 50 feet in girth. Upon two colossal frog legs, a huge rhinoceros head and a dragon's mouth leered hungrily down at them. "I am FROG, the Fearless Receptionist Of Gods. To whom shall I refer you?"

Everyone looked to Miguel, for he had somehow assumed command of this unholy quest, and Miguel, on the verge of crying, looked upon the mighty monstrosity above him. "Uhh... We're looking for God?"

Flames ripped uncontrollably out of FROG's gaping maw, and bathed the group in fiery doom. They scattered and dodged as best as they could, and though they leapt up into battle-stances soon afterward, they ended up confused as FROG jerked about, nearly rolling around before them.

It appeared as if FROG was laughing... "You newbies! Go 250 miles that way, and turn left."

And at that they noticed the flames had burned a massive arrow upon the ground. Listening to the living Rolodex, they traveled the great distance, and now found themselves at a hut of oversized proportions. Hundreds of serfs in white robes struggled outside the huge hovel. Many were riding in wagons overflowing with meats of various types, while others still were riding wagons that were really big flagons overflowing with wine. The starving adventurers, as they had been subsisting only on dried meats in nobody knows how long, they all temporarily forgot their quest, and felt only the pangs of hunger and the want for blood and wine.

After slaying a few random serfs with such ease that it made their mouths water, they gorged themselves upon the meat of a wagon.

"Uhhh.... Guys. I don't think this was such a good idea." Ethnocentric Dracula chimed in, after sucking one of the rarer pieces of meat dry.

El Krunko put down his half of a lamb, and looked up. "Huh?"

E.D. pointed towards the hut, and the four of them froze in shock. Stumbling out of the hovel was a creature more horrific than Mr. Horror. It was ugly beyond words, larger than life, and smellier than Happy Barrypants. And it wore a wife-beater with words hastily writ in wine on the front that read, "I am Garguantuanly Obese Dwarf. And YOU are NOT."

"Ok... So what's the big deal?" El Krunko shrugged... And that's when he saw it.

The words, "Newbie Killer," were scrawled on his mansion sized battleaxe hilt.

"Isn't that what FROG called us?" Happy queried. "Newbies?"

"If he asks... I don't know any of you."

And at that, Miguel Sanchez ran back to hell.

TABLET: LXXIII

Ethnocentric Dracula pondered for a moment, then cried out to GOD. "Ah Ah Ah.... You realize your existence is a paradox; being both Gargantuan and a Dwarf!" GOD reflected on this, and a moment later shrieked out in pain as he shriveled into nothing.

"Well then!" El Krunko bellowed out. "GOD was kinda a pussy, now wasn't he? I bet there's a whole lot more satisfying things to slay around here."

So the three roamed about the plains where Gods lived, slaying them in battles to which hymns are still sung in reverence of.

Like: (to the tune of, "Twinkle Twinkle Little Star.")

> El Krunko
> El Krunko
> He killed stuff
>
> Lots
> And lots
> Of stuff
>
> Things went down
> They went down hard
> Went down like Godly sacks of lard
>
> El Krunko
> El Krunko
> He killed stuff
>
> Lots
> And lots
> Of stuff

And other timeless classics like: (to the tune of, "Old McDonald.")

> Ethnocentric Dracula
> Crushed some Gods
> EIEIO
>
> He crushed them all up with his mauls
> EIEIO

With a CRUNCH SPLAT here
And a CRUNCH SUCK there

Here a SUCK
There a SPLAT
Everywhere a SUCK SPLAT!

Ethnocentric Dracula
Crushed some Gods
EIEIO

And who could forget: (to the tune of, "Strawberry Fields.")

Happy's gonna take you down
In these here,
Crimson Death Fields
Everything's dead

There's corpses and stuff all strung about

Crimson Death Fields forever...

Of notable slaying, Happy Barrypants slew Prince Rainbow. Because of this, any weapon Happy swings leaves a rainbow trail, as does any spaceship he travels upon.

Ethnocentric Dracula utterly annihilated a being known to its parishioners as Gluttonous Maximus, the Fattest thing in all creation! When Ethnocentric Dracula reduced this being to fatty offal, he had learned to change his size and density at will.

And of most merit and grander, El Krunko slew two notable Gods. The lesser of these achievements was the slaying of Lord Slay. For this, El Krunko now dons the title, "El Krunko: Lord of the Slay!"

The most heralded, and to date the most Epic battle that had ever occurred took place between El Krunko: Lord of the Slay, and Surfius: Greek God of Surfing. This battle raged over 40 days and 40 nights; each contender locked in mortal combat while surfing around the world, again and again. When El Krunko stood victorious he had gained the ability to surf ANYTHING, and took as his trophy Surfius' Intergalactic Ancestral Surfboard, better known as the I.A.S. El Krunko swore to never let that treasure leave his side.

Many other Gods fell privy to the three's unstoppable carnival of carnage, leaving so many lost sheep out there in the Universe with their prayers falling upon dead ears. In fact, it was this very thing that truly inspired the trio. Content with their power trip, the three made their way back to the LGOD reception desk so that they might find Miguel Sanchez Clone TK-421 and gloat about their many victories over some much needed booze.

TABLET: LXXIV

When they reached the Dark Lord's land, they discovered him reclining on a sofa, being fed peeled grapes by one of his many voluptuous handmaidens. Miguel Sanchez played pinball off to the side while he waited for them.

"Tres bien!" Satan said when they approached. For Satan it was necessary to speak with a difference accent each day of the week. "So, God est morte, no?"

"Indeed," El Krunko replied imperiously. "And

now you must assist us."

"Oui. As you say, a bargain is a bargain."

But just then, a buxom blonde handmaiden rushed into the room. "My Lord," she cried. "GOD has just been seen wandering the hills, looking for the entrance to Hell! He means to engage you in Mortal Kombat ™!"

Satan was furious beyond words. "Deceivers! You did not destroy the Goofy Old Dragon, as was our bargain!" A ball of fire emerged from his hand, and he raised it ready to bathe the four heroes in burning flame.

"Goofy Old Dragon?" E.D. quacked. "We killed the Gargantuan Obese Dwarf."

Satan's expression of grim determination and unearthly rage slowly melted, and his angry face transformed into one of mirth. Soon he couldn't help himself but to laugh, and before long everyone in the room was chuckling heartily.

"You killed the wrong God!" Satan said, and they all laughed anew.

TABLET: LXXV

And so they all laughed, and laughed together. Soon, amidst the hilarity of the frabjous scene, it seemed as if Satan and the heroes were not merely acquaintances, but actual friends, perhaps even family. As everyone went on chuckling in hysterics, Happy Barrypants paused and took a somber moment to reflect on that thought, as well as even go so far as to reconsider his opinion on the Eternal Lord of Darkness.

Perhaps I have been too hasty at calling him off

as a murderous fiend that was only using me for my fiendishly murderous desires. Happy thought. *Maybe this Satan guy isn't such a bad dude after all.* And with that, Happy finally knew what he had to do if he was ever to complete what he had begun so many aeons ago, when it was dark. "Satan!" he screamed at the top of his lungs.

Satan, half-stifling his chuckles, managed to reply with a, "Oui monsieur?"

Happy stood up. "Oh mighty Satan. I offer you my undying soul in exchange for the power to defeat my... well, my undying arch-nemesis." He clenched his fist in the air, and shook it, as if challenging the sky. "Gribulor! The Great Goat-Man!"

El Krunko and the others fell deathly silent "Pffffft..." Satan burst into laughter.

A good 20 minutes went by before they were able to rouse him from his manic fit and get a legible response, but as he was about to speak, the same buxom blonde handmaiden came into the room, with an even more urgent message. "My Lord, GOD has invoked his Godly powers to lure your many denizens into the hills to face him. Even now he screams obscenities, awaiting you to accept his challenge. My Lord! The rivers of the upper world bleed with the contents of Hell itself! My Lord! Hell has emptied itself, and we are left defenseless!" At this point she put her hands on her pig-tails, ran circles round the heroes shrilling and shrieking screams most foul.

"Satan!" El Krunko surfed up into the air and spun his Ancestral Chainsaw in circles on his pinky finger. "My mission is clear. We may have failed in our quest to kill GOD, but allow us to re-slay all of Hell, and send them back to Hell!" Satan fell down from his mighty pedestal, in another fit of laughter. It was the thumbs up which gave El Krunko the go-ahead. Miguel Sanchez back flipped towards the exit, and E.D. ran to catch up.

El Krunko put his hand on Happy Barrypants shoulder, and looked with a hard stare into Happy Barrypants eyes. "Fellow Green Pig Legendary Hero. Fellow slayer of stuff. Come with me now, on what will surely be our most carnage filled day!"

Tears filled Happy's left eye, and the other blinked wildly. Yes, it was destiny alright. El Krunko surfed out of the room, and Happy was about to follow, when he realized Satan had never given him an answer regarding help with Gribulor. He walked up to the Lord of Lies, and put his hands on his hips. "Well, what about it?"

Satan stifled his laughter in one quick cry, and looked down upon the living legend. "Monsieur, I cannot. Gribulor gave me his first born, and until GOD is dead, it's first come, first serve. Pardon e' moi. Bon soir."

TABLET: LXXVI

As the group once again existed the gates of Hell, El Krunko suggested the four stop for some doughnuts and tea (after all, they had been out slaughtering for many moons). Right nearby was a conveniently placed a Dunkin' Donuts. Inside the four of them ordered 2 dozen donuts and four large cups of tea.

El Krunko was the first to speak. "I'm sorry gentlemen, but I just have to say it. I don't like this Satan business. No sir, not one bit. He's gonna just keep jerkin' us around doing his busy work."

The group nodded in agreement as they ate their donuts and sipped their tea. Happy Barrypants finally tossed his empty cup aside (and left a rainbow trail in doing so), and retorted, "So we're serving the Lord of Lies, big deal. I want MY REVENGE." At this point Happy was standing up and waving his arms about in a fit of welled up rage against Gribulor.

Miguel Sanchez chimed in, "Well... We've got nothing better to do," and shrugged.

El Krunko sighed. "If it's idle questing you're looking for, I know a machine on Chronos 4 that–"

Happy cut him off. "I feel like all I've been doing is idle questing. I want to do some thing meaningful in this Universe". Everyone at the table nodded as the four dozen donuts dwindled.

A moment went by, and Miguel calmly stated, "I've got something. We could create an institution that recruits volunteers to build homes for the less fortunate of the cosmos. We could call it, 'Habitat for Humanity, and Stuff.' " Everyone at the table nodded as Ethnocentric Dracula ate the last Boston creme.

El Krunko slammed down his empty Styrofoam container. "It's settled then." And the four walked out of Dunkin Donuts for the last time.

TABLET: LXXVII

They strode by the plain of battle, where GOD was busy slaying the minions of Hell by the dozens. But as each one fell, endless additional waves of evil spirits, malicious ghosts, and unhappy demons came pouring from the nearby gates. For the first time in his short, adventure-filled life, Happy held no desire to join in on the bloody carnage. Taking his lead, the companions ventured west and left the land where the entrance to Hell was located, of which I will say nothing more, lest young, impressionable children seek it out, end up being sucked into its terrible depths, and their parents end up suing the teller of this tale.

As they continued onward, seeking those who required their assistance, Happy realized, for the first time in his life, that his name was not a misnomer: he was, indeed, happy. He began humming a joyous tune, and skipping around his friends, and picking colorful wild flowers and tossing them about.

"What the fuck are you doing?" Ethnocentric Dracula demanded.

"Well," Happy explained. "You know how you've always felt Ethnocentric? I finally understand why you felt so complete in your existence. For I am now both Happy... and happy!" He beamed with joy.

"But," E.D. replied, "Your name isn't actually Happy. It's Barry."

TABLET: LXXVIII

Miguel Sanchez dropped his mocha latte on the floor in shock, and nearly choked on the last bite of his penultimate leftover strawberry jammie. "You're Barry Happypants!!?" he shouted at the top of his lungs, as everyone shut up and looked warily at him.

"Umm... well I prefer Happy. 'Specially now that I'm so happy these days, and all, and it's ever so fitting. But yes, that is who I once was, what I think might have been many aeons ago, but I can't be so sure, because–"

Miguel Sanchez interrupted him. "Quiet fool. I

have a message for you."

El Krunko whispered in E.D.'s ear, "I thought that pig's name sounded familiar. But I thought Barry Happypants was killed by Gribulor? I saw him one time at the museum."

Ethnocentric Dracula quietly spoke in El Krunko's ear. "He was. Shhh."

Miguel stepped back, and started fishing through his pocket, while Happy mindlessly noshed on the bag of Baco-Cruncho's he picked up from a vending machine a few minutes earlier. He'd toss them in the air, and follow their nifty rainbow trails into his mouth. "Rainbow power kicks ass," he declared.

Miguel spoke as searched his pockets... "One of my many clones questfully took on an Epic quest, and when he failed, I swore vengeance to avenge his death, and complete what he had begun, but had not done. I thought the chance would never arise, but now it finally has! And I, TK-421, will surely succeed where so many Sanchii have failed in the past, because of failure!" The other three heroes had no idea what he was talking about, and impatiently waited for him to get to the point. Miguel Sanchez smiled as his hand finally gripped what he had been hastily searching for in his coat pockets. "The death of Barry Happypants! FOR GRIBULOR!" At this, he revealed a shiny plaid orb.

Ethnocentric Dracula shouted out in horrified horribleness. "He's holding a Germal Detonator!!!" Miguel Sanchez gleefully laughed in glee.

"There's enough germs in there to wipe out this entire quadrant of the galaxy!" El Krunko cried.

"Yes!" Clone TK-421 answered. "And it's set to pig..."

"But I'm not actually a–"

"Shhh..." Miguel Sanchez Clone TK-421 silenced El Krunko with a finger over his lips. "El Krunko, I never meant to harm you. But when you really think about it, what more fitting an end, than for both legendary Green Pig heroes to be annihilated by the clone of El Krunko's mortal enemy, Miguel Sanchez, who has also taken on the quest of Gribulor, Barry Happypants' mortal enemy!? It's a shame that I will perish as well, but I won't be dead for long, as Gribulor will surely resurrect me again in the invisible clone tube probe, the Sanchinator, lead by none other than Sancho the Unstoppable Sanchez, and his Sanchii royal guard. They've been following us around this entire time! Ever since we left the time-chamber!"

Miguel Sanchez Clone TK-421 flipped on a switch that had been cleverly disguised as a wart on his left cheek, and a gigantic slate-grey platform uncloaked in the skies above them. Hundreds and thousands of Miguel Sanchii stood upon it, each and every one of them wearing numbered tunics, and every last one and sipping identically prepared Mocha Latte's.

El Krunko gaped in astonished. "TK-4211, TK-4212... TK42.. Awesome! I'm gonna have SO MANY SIDEKICKS!"

Happy Barrypants dropped to his knees, raised his hands up at Miguel, and pleaded with him. "Don't do it Miguel. You don't know what you're saying. What about our glorious plans for the Habitat for Humanity and Stuff? Don't you want to help people?"

Miguel Sanchez Clone TK-421's conviction began to falter. "Yes... I do. Truly I do... But what else am I to do? What can I do? I can't help it! I must complete my quest!"

Happy cried aloud. "No! Don't you realize?

You're not like that anymore. You've changed! You were reborn in Hell! You're not like that anymore! You're not the same clone as you were back then. Thing's are all different now! TK-421 walked into Hell that day, and you know who came out? TK-42NEW."

Miguel stumble backwards. "But... but... no!! No! No! Never! I MUST END THIS BLOODY CONFLICT ONCE AND FOR ALL! The last two Green Pig heroes will be no more!"

In a flurry of Styrofoam cups, the Miguel Sanchii guard began to parachute down from the floating platform, while others took to the air in hand gliders and rocket packs. Some of the low-toner clones got too excited and just jumped off the platform, falling to their doom, when suddenly, THUMP! The clone of Miguel Sanchez TK-421 standing before them was crushed beneath a big black box. It bore the markings, "Intergalactic Insta-safe. Fares on inside door. Guaranteed safe travel! This side up!" The safe door swung open, only to reveal the Green Pig Langust, and fellow Green Pig Grunta-Grunta-Pow-Wow, and some sort of robotic contraption with a cannon for a head, guns for arms, and swords for legs (of which is had 5).

"Not 2, but 4 Green Pig heroes!" Langust grinned.

"Am I late?" Grunt-Grunta-Pow-Wow inquired.

"No... You're right on time." El Krunko smiled. Yes, his decision to skip the battle of Hell was a foolish one, but perhaps he could go back later. For now, Sanchii were on his mind. "How many millions of them could be on board that floating platform?" he asked to no one in particular, as the gang readied their Ancestral Weaponry ™.

The robot leapt out of the safe, and without

introducing itself, unleashed an endless barrage of anti-aircraft fire into the air. "I'm gonna wack those meatbags!" it said in standard robo-monotone. Ethnocentric Dracula grinned in satisfaction, for it was already established he had a thing for robots, especially murderous ones.

TABLET: LXXIX

The battle had begun. The three heroes (that is, Happy, E.D. and El Krunko, as by now E.D. had long since proven his heroism), and their new-found sidekicks, fought with a fury and determination that the Universe rarely sees. Wave after wave of cloned Miguel Sanchii were cut down, blown apart, and bashed to smithereens, yet wave after wave continued to bear down upon them. They came by massive transport ships, huge armored red cars, and enormous hovercraft, and were efficiently stacked into each, so that not one foot of space was wasted. Slash! Boom! Smack! Crush! The bodies of the clones piled high, and soon none of the combatants stood on solid ground any longer, but trod through the bodies of the fallen as if wading through a thick swamp.

Days and nights past, and yet no headway was being made, for still the Sanchii came in a seemingly endless swarm. Where once the sky was a light blue, it was now marred by the haze of war and buzzed with the roar of jet engines. Determination, slowly but surely, gave way to exhaustion, and fury to gut-wrenching anguish. But still they came, wave after wave. Happy watched helplessly as the two Green Pig warriors, Langust and Grunta-Grunta-Pow-Wow, succumbed to the Sanchii, and were ripped to bloody shreds. Soon after, Ethnocentric Dracula was enveloped by a swarm of foes, and Happy could no longer see any sign of his ally. Even El Krunko, whose pile of slain enemies was greater than any other, was having difficulty. He gritted his teeth, sweat pored down his brow, and fresh blood covered the gore that was already caked over him. And deep within El Krunko's raging eyes, Happy could see the embers of despair growing; the realization that perhaps, as unimaginable as it might be, this would be El Krunko's *final battle*.

Happy wept in sadness, and fear, and shame, that the carnage around him would soon claim the life of his last living Green Pig ally. But suddenly, inspiration struck! It's hard to say whether the Gods took pity on Happy's plight, or if the adrenaline in his system rushed to his brain at an opportune moment, or if he finally chose to burn the last 15 brain cells he had been storing, or maybe even the spirit of Sing Potato suggested it to him. No matter. Happy leapt forward, and cried out at the top of his lungs, and with all the strength that was left in him, "$ab((a+b)/b)$."

Miguel Sanchez TK-241, who was in charge of this particular phase of the operation, suddenly froze. His face grew pale, his mouth drooped, and he shouted in anger. "Nooooooooooooo!" For as soon as his clones heard the formula uttered from Happy's mouth, they were instantly destroyed. As sound traveled over the plain of battle, clones simultaneously disintegrated as if made of nothing but ash, burst into flames as if spontaneously combusting, and exploded in showers of muscle and blood, as if placed in a microwave by a sadistic red-haired child, you know, the soulless kind. All that remained was a mountain of corpses and body parts... and silence.

The wind whistled in the air.

Miguel's war machines now stood still, their passengers destroyed, and their thrusters disabled.

Happy, El Krunko and TK-241 stood staring at one another, as the quiet wind blew across the gore-soaked land.

TABLET: LXXX

Happy's left ear twitched. As the cool breeze brushed past his battle-torn body, and a pristine calm crept across the razed wasteland, Happy's senses pushed outward, looking for anything living to focus upon. Beyond the dusty swamp fields, over the endless quiet forest and brush-land, skirting the untraveled barrens and the unloved zone of death, well past the ancient forgotten libraries, and just left of Schmitt's Home for the Mute, he felt a presence that blared stronger than anywhere else.

Without thinking, and certainly without paying attention to what he was doing, Happy Barrypants, the Legendary Green Pig Hero with a tattoo on his left testicle from the Red Monkey Prophet, who was complete with Red Monkey Shaman metal endo-skeleton action, wielding an Ancestral Shotgun, an Ancestral Ammo Bandolier, and, who formerly could not fly, leapt up into the air, and in all of his cool Rainbow Brite-esque glory, started flying in that direction. You know, towards Schmitt's.

El Krunko clutched his Ancestral Chainsaw tight, and spit a wad of chewin' flesh onto the ground. To him, it appeared as if Happy Barrypants had merely gone irreversibly insane as a result of being unable to handle the carnage. "No big surprise for El Krunko:

Lord of the Slay," he said to himself, as his eyes narrowed and took in the spectacle before him. Tens of thousands of jet packs, hundreds of thousands of ground vehicles, and an uncountable plethora of arms, missiles, and other projectile weapons littered the battlefield, all beneath the cold shadow of the immense fortress, the Sanchinator, above them.

Deep within his impenetrable Sanchii Sanctuary, Sancho The Unstoppable Sanchez majestically paced the Abyssal Walkway. "It is unfortunate that one of the heroes placed within Oubliette X was theorem conscious, but it still does not interfere with our agenda." He turned, walked dramatically towards the Obelisk of Uncertainty, and pointed fiercely at it.

"I will not be made fool of, and damned be the council! I'll handle these vagrants and be done with it. Leave everything to me!" He turned again, and knelt before the camera, stretching his arms outward. "Forgive me this one callous act, but I'm taking control of the entire army! All around the galaxy, people will quiver in sympathy for me, and what I must do."

"El Krunko!" TK-241 laughed. "Your friend may have eradicated my TK-421 series. But can you defeat a TK-421 series, without a TK-421 series?" TK-241 flicked a few switches on his remote control.

"What do you mean!?" El Krunko bellowed out as he surfed across the endless mountains of mechanical debris to get closer to the last remaining Sanchez.

The lone clone raised remote control, which was now glowing with its own battery powered splendor, high above his head and screamed, "Invisible Sanchez Mechano-Clone Attack!!!"

... El Krunko waited, but nothing seemed to happen. TK-241 froze, and slowly lowered the remote control as its blue glow faded away.

El Krunko surfed up beside him and revved up his A.C. "Looks like your tech ain't gonna save you this time, scumbag. I don't know where you or your damned Sanchez came from, but eat hellish bliss! If you're lucky, I won't slay you twice like I gotta do to everyone else."

TK-241's face contorted, and he looked up confused. "You... You don't remember? You don't remember the Army of the Sanchii? But that's ..."

Alas, before he could finish his sentence, his head was chopped off. El Krunko spit on the corpse, and crushed the controller beneath his boot heel.

With that task finished, El Krunko picked up speed and surfed the metal hills looking for his lost allies.

"Ethnocentric Dracula!!! Where are you?" he cried out into the wastelands.

"Here I am!" a voice cried out.

El Krunko spun his IAS in circles, but he couldn't find the source. "Where?" he called out.

"Over here! I turned into this sink to get out a pickle." Ethnocentric poofed into existence.

"Oh yeah. Right. I forgot you killed that God fatty, or whatever. What do you think, should we go find Happy, or go up there," he pointed at the floating citadel, "and waste them all?"

Ethnocentric Dracula shook his head and grinned maniacally. "Happy shmappy. How bout you and I take over that thing, and fly ourselves off of this fucking planet. What was that place you mentioned? The one with the most beautiful women in the world?"

El Krunko smiled. "You mean the moon of Ger? Why?"

E.D. picked his tooth. "My good man. If I'm going to hunt down all who are different, I might as well start with them."

All around them the ground rumbled, and the debris mountains shook.

"WHAT'S GOING ON"!" El Krunko roared mightily, as all the remaining unmanned machines powered up.

TABLET: LXXXI

Meanwhile, Happy was speeding through the mountains, already having passed the Mystical Mountain, the Magical Mountain, the Mystical Magical Mountain Monastery, and the Mountain of Mythical Mayhem. He flew right over some ancient library, which caused the pages of open books to flutter uncontrollably, disturbing the many scholars examining them. Soon he slowed, and as he neared the Home for the Mute, he felt the strange presence was close. But when he finally stood upon the very spot from which the strange energy was emanating, nothing was to be found.

Then... slowly... A shimmering form appeared before him.

It was an orb, strangely familiar to his sight, and it glew a primordial green.

"The orb of the Drunken Wanderer!" Happy whispered. He cautiously reached out and grasped it. His hands clung to the orb as if attracted by some magnetic force. A power coursed through him causing his hair to stand on end. Images flashed in his mind. Images of the ancient past, of the tale of Lothar Happypants and Briguvor, images of his own past, as a mercenary assassin, trained by the Og Corp. and oft hired by the unscrupulous leaders of the Red Monkey civilization. Then came visions of the future, when Gribulor the Great Goat-Man would face him in final, earth-shattering combat.

When the shock of power stopped, Happy blacked out.

But he knew, deep within the dark recesses of his unconscious mind, that he had finally found the strength to defeat Gribulor.

How that strength would manifest itself, however, was still a mystery to him.

TABLET: LXXXII

Ethnocentric Dracula hopped onto El Krunko's surfboard and hastily attempted to formulate a plan. "There's just too many of them!" All around them, hundreds of thousands of ground vehicles slowly encroached in on their position, while in the skies above the tens of thousands of jet-packs roared furiously as they hovered overhead and awaited whatever command would cause them to attack.

"That's it man! It's game over man! Game over!" E.D. cried out in panic. "How do we fight an enemy that doesn't exist!?" He flapped his duck wings in gestures that pointed at the empty pilot seats of the nearest fleet of hovercrafts. "How do we fight on, when everyone to fight is already dead! It's madness! There's nothing left out there to destroy but sheer weaponry! It's insane!" E.D. dropped to his knees and clutched at thin air as he sobbed for the first time in his shallow ethnocentric life.

El Krunko surfed down to the barren center of

one of the revving tank valleys, and whipping out his Ancestral Chainsaw, hopped off onto the ground. As he landed he tried to rev it and make intimidating gestures at the approaching wall of imminent death, but his A.C. was out of juice, and refused to start.

"It looks like we make our last stand!" El Krunko laughed. So as to spit on the first tank he'd face, he balled up his reserve saliva, and considered the situation.

"Langust and Grunta-Grunta-Pow-Wow are dead," he said to E.D. without making eye contact. "Happy Barrypants has turned chicken again and fled. Miguel Sanchez Clone TK-421 was nothing but a TK-42 phony. And now you, the mighty Ethnocentric Dracula that even slew some random God is showing his true colors..." El Krunko spit his reserve saliva at his feet in a show of his macho-ness. "It always comes down to El Krunko and his trusty Ancestral Chainsaw, doesn't it? What did that scumbag mean anyway, when he said I didn't remember? The Sanchii... Have I... faced them before? Why can't I remember!?"

El Krunko closed his eyes and took a deep breath. "I guess it doesn't matter anymore..." He slung his spent Ancestral Chainsaw over his back and cracked his knuckles. "This is gonna take fuckin' forever..."

The machines began the attack.

Just then, at their darkest hour, as missiles flew and bullets sang, and as El Krunko was about to say, "This is fuckin' bullshit, I'm outta here!" but never got the opportunity, it happened...

All around the duo, laser beams erupted from the ground! Amidst the frenzy of projectiles and ensuing explosions, they fell down, and fell far. Rock and stone assailed the two of them as if missiles of their own, the pieces falling upwards into them as they careened deeper into crater dug by the barrage of laser fire. 30 seconds. 60 seconds. 90 seconds! It began to get unnecessarily deep and repetitive.

Just as El Krunko wondered just how deep he would fall before he would say, "This is fuckin bullshit, I'm outta here!" as he had originally intended, and surf back up to his shoe-in doom out of sheer boredom alone, gravity waves encompassed them, and they were stopped short enough to prevent their careening into the sky, and softly enough to take in the awesome spectacle before them as they landed upside-down on the ground. There they sat, on the other side of the Goat Home-world's crust.

Far above them, the strange Purple Sun gleamed in the center of the planet.

Many thousands of miles in the distance, beyond the green seas and the blue forests, lay a colossal spire that shimmered as if of pure gold ,and climbed into the sun. While ever so much closer to them and looming in the foreground was the robotic monstrosity that had exited the safe alongside Langust and G.G.P.W.

"Greetings meat-bags," it said in standard robo-monotone. "I am HK-48, and my master Langust got thrashed by those other meat-bags. You're my new master now El Krunko, and our first duty is carnage-filled revenge, and possibly an attempt at resurrecting Langust with my regeneration gun... and possibly an attempt at resurrecting all the meat-bags, so as to murdelize them a second time, and then possibly an attempt at resurrecting all the meat-bags, so as to waste em' a third time too, for good measure."

The robot hopped up and down, and spun its

sword-like legs in circles, and shot random fire into the air. "Areeba! Areeba!" it beeped and blooped.

El Krunko shrugged. "Alright. Let's go."

Ethnocentric Dracula stood up, and pointed down, which would be up if you were on the other side of the Goat Home-world's crust. "Uhh, guys? I don't think we need to go anywhere."

"Oh, no?" El Krunko inquired. "And why's that?"

"Because they're coming to us!" And he was right, for all the machines of war had driven into the hole too, and were about to emerge above them, or below them, depending on perspective.

TABLET: LXXXIII

Meanwhile, as El Krunko and Ethnocentric Dracula were preparing for battle yet again, Happy was elsewhere, and his eyes were fluttering open. All was bright around him, but soon his eyes adjusted, and he found himself in a forest of sorts. The sounds of tribal chanting carried along the wind. The words and beats were rhythmic, but their tone was shrill and high pitched.

His curiosity aroused, Happy arose, and made his way through the wood. He soon came across a clearing. There in the center of the mysterious glade was a pit of fire, flame-a-blazin', with five Red Monkeys chanting words of praise to their God, the Great Grape Ape, who dwelt in the Jungle Heaven.

When Happy appeared, the monkeys suddenly stopped, and turned towards him. One came forward and pointed a thin, bent finger at the hero.

"Barry Happypants," it croaked, "do you not

remember me, the Red Monkey Shaman Higgle-de?"

Impossible, Happy thought. *This cannot be Higgle-de, for when I met him last, he was young and full of vigor.*

"I hear the words in your mind," the Shaman said. "I have grown strong with age, and my magical talents have increased tenfold since last we met. The secret of how to traverse time and space instantaneously is in my hand, but I was foolish... and I did not realize that even when one travels to another time... one still ages normally... But no matter."

A sign! Happy thought. *Perhaps this is the way I will defeat Gribulor!*

"I know nothing of that," the Red Monkey Shaman said.

Then what help is he to me?

"I will reunite you with your companions, who even now prepare for *yet another* dire battle of Epic proportions!"

Hmmm... An expression of puzzlement came over Happy's face. *I wonder what happened to them, that they have started a new Epic battle without me?*

"'Tis wondrous strange, that tale," the RMS replied to Happy's thoughts.

Suddenly, Happy was seized with a murderous rage. He grasped the RMS's head with one hand, his body with the other, and twisted as hard as he could. The sound of snapping bone and twisting tissue echoed through the quiet glade, and the other Red Monkeys screeched and howled.

"Bet you didn't know I was thinking about that!" Happy yelled at the Shaman's corpse.

TABLET: LXXXIV

The Red Monkeys inched towards Happy with death in their eyes, while he stood there triumphant, drenched in their master's ichor.

Just as battle was about to ensue, a diamond shaped portal appeared beside Higgle-de's corpse, and out stepped El Krunko and Ethnocentric Dracula, each sporting long beards.

Before anyone could react, the two newcomers promptly slew the Red Monkeys.

"Great Gribulor's Ghost!" Happy shouted and shook his fists. "Who are you? And why do you look like my friends?"

El Krunko slung his Ancestral Chainsaw across his back, and heroically pointed off to the distance. "We are from an alternate time-line that should not exist, but was created only seconds ago, according to our calculations, when you slew the Red Monkey Shaman."

"Without his power," Ethnocentric Dracula quacked, "the Universe is completely doomed."

Happy took two steps closer. "Why should I believe you?"

"You'd believe El Krunko, wouldn't you?" El Krunko said. "So then why should you not believe us?"

"Because you're not El Krunko!" Happy explained.

"Ahh, but I *am* El Krunko too." El Krunko retorted.

Meanwhile, El Krunko The First was in battle pose, catching his breath before the next round of combat, as the hordes of war machines spewed forth from the chasm like an unholy mechanical geyser of certain death. That's when the ground shook violently.

Ethnocentric Dracula pointed to the huge golden spire in the far distance, where it had cracked, and was careening upward into the Purple Sun. "Something's happening!"

"El Krunko II eh?" Happy scratched his chin. "But where's *my* El Krunko?"

"Right where I've been pointing... this entire time!" he bellowed.

BOOOOOM! Night turned to day, and when Happy looked to where El Krunko II was pointing, he saw a mushroom cloud burst into the sky. "MY FRIENDS!!! NOOOO!!!!"

Ethnocentric Dracula II leapt forward and put Happy in a headlock. "There's no time for this E.K. My scanner's picking up a fluctuation." Beep! Boop! E.D. II's pocket-watch was sounding an alarm. "I'm activating the time matrix now!"

E.D. II quacked at a specific frequency, and as the three of them dematerialized, in their place another time-portal appeared. Out stepped El Krunko III, who sported a goatee, and Ethnocentric Dracula III, who donned 3 mauls in each of his 3 hands.

Happy and his phony cohorts rematerialized in giant large warehouse that was literally overflowing with electronic equipment.

"Where are we?" Happy asked El Krunko II as he struggled free from the headlock.

"We are deep within the halls of the resistance fortress. When you slew the Red Monkey Shaman the planet tore itself to shreds and detonated in a really cool explosion. However, in an alternate time-line, Ethnocentric Dracula and I were spared death, as we chose to flee the Sanchii on my IAS, and surfed to the moon of Ger, where the most beautiful women in the

Universe are known to be."

El Krunko II approached a dusty console, and had it materialize some ice cold brewskies. Ethnocentric Dracula II continued where El Krunko II had left off. "We spent only 3 weeks with the girls, but in that time, Gribulor had learned of your destruction, and with it, there was nothing to prevent him from galactic domination. His horrible empire and its creations have overrun every planet there is. It's taken us over 45 years of searching, but we've finally discovered the means to end Grand Emperor Gribulor's tyrannical reign of terror."

El Krunko II shook his beer can at Happy. "We found out the whole reason we're in this mess is because of you Happy! You fucked everything up, and now we have to take you back in time, and bring an end to our own existence, just to save the Universe!" He rolled his eyes and groaned with annoyance. "But it still beats the hell out of living our lives as slaves to a goat."

Without warning the metal ceiling above them melted away, and huge sentinel-like metallic monstrosities hovered down on their booster jet boots, and littered the warehouse in laser fire. They were humanoid, and had no visible weaponry, but their eyes glowed red and shot laser beams, their arms shot missiles out of nowhere, and they were very, very scary looking. Ethnocentric Dracula II pummeled Happy and knocked him out of the way of a rogue missile, while El Krunko II leapt into the fray.

"It's Gribulor's Hero Hunters!" E.K. II grunted. "How the hell did they find us here!? There must be a traitor in the resistance!"

E.D. II cried out in typical terror, but El Krunko II was not so easily frightened. He karate chopped the leg of one of the beasts and ripped it in half. The creature, unable to support itself, crumbled to the floor and exploded. El Krunko II ducked, weaved, and bobbed, keeping himself clear of the lasers and grenades, as he smashed the butt of his alternate Ancestral Chainsaw on a second Hunter's boot. The Hunter leapt to the air as its battle protocols dictated, but El Krunko II was ready. With one mighty swing he heroically beheaded the Hero Hunter once and for all. As the thing landed it fell backwards and exploded, littering the room with dangerous shrapnel that bounced harmlessly off of El Krunko II's powerful beard.

But their victory was short lived.

Fifteen other Hero Hunters melted their way into the sub-level, and descended to take the place of the two that had fallen.

"There's too many of them!" El Krunko II growled.

"Then perhaps, you should surrender," a deep voice echoed.

"It... It can't be!" Ethnocentric Dracula II cried out, and seemed a duck on the verge of insanity.

El Krunko II shed a single tear, then leaned over, and puked.

TABLET: LXXXV

Happy's eyes gazed towards the heavens, but before he could see from whence the voice issued, he slipped on El Krunko II's puke, and fell flat on his face, breaking his nose in the process. "Ouchy!" he cried out.

"That voice..." the voice said. "That voice! It... No... It cannot be!"

Ethnocentric Dracula and El Krunko (or rather,

their alternate time-line counterparts), looked up with hope, for it seemed that for the first time in their long struggle, they heard fear in the voice of Multinational Mummyman, Gribulor's most feared operative. Whether it was out of genuine fear or merely surprise, they could not yet tell. Happy spun around from where he lay on the floor, his face covered in bright red blood and olive green vomit. He laughed when he saw his foe, and sprang to his feet. "Bah!" he exclaimed. "Multinational Mummyman? I've slain this jerk-off twice already!"

Happy leapt into the air, dodged every last laser blast that flew at him from the eyes of the Hero Hunters, and landed on the roof the resistance's headquarters.

El Krunko II slapped E.D. II across the face. "Snap out of it man!" he shouted. "We've gotta fight these robots to give Happy enough time to defeat Multinational Mummyman!"

Ethnocentric Dracula II grasped his feathered hands in fury, and proclaimed, "Indeed. These Hero Hunters have stolen my ethnocentric thunder for long enough. To arms!" With that, he raised his mauls and brought them down upon the feet of the nearest robot.

The robot cried out in agony, "001011101010100011001!" and fell to the ground, where E.D. II promptly bashed its head to pieces with one maul, while blocking a laser blast with the other. El Krunko II, spurred on by his comrade's display of martial prowess, leapt into the air and started carving through the Hero Hunters with his Ancestral Chainsaw II. A few of the robots were caught off guard by the furious assault, which did not compute, and their synapses were instantly fried.

Happy, meanwhile, stood on the roof, looking around the blasted landscape. "So this is the metaphoric crop, that Gribulor metaphorically sowed, and then metaphorically reaped," he whispered. "I shall destroy Gribulor in each and every dimension if need be, for he is my true and eternal enemy! But first... I will destroy you Multinational Mummyman!"

But the villain was nowhere to be seen.

TABLET: LXXXVI

Our intertimensional hero, Happy Barrypants, walked to the edge of the roof in order to get a better look at the spectacle of the future landscape. However post-apocalyptic it might have appeared at first glance, Happy had still expected to see hover-mobiles, flying delivery vending machines, and a plethora of other supra-high tech mechanical creations. What he instead viewed knocked the wind out of him, and he puked over the side of the Headquarters.

On the horizon, the dual violet suns of Glendor'ah'bah were just rising, and they illuminated the megalithic city scape with their soft glow. Countless skyscrapers littered the skies with their metallic majesty, and innumerable hover-mobiles scattered about just as Happy had predicted, but this was not what turned his stomach. Hundreds of thousands of people wandered the streets beginning an average day in their average lives.... But every single one of them, every single last one of them, was Miguel Sanchez! Happy's eyes welled with tears.

Happy tried to scream, but his voice eluded him. He couldn't help but stare in awe as the suns lit the land and illuminated the unholy capital of the neo-Sanchii metropolis. Floating motionlessly above the largest and most expensive of the towers was the Sanchinator Fortress, and he knew it by name thanks to its massive neon green billboard sign.

Ethnocentric Dracula II and El Krunko II pushed open the fire escape doors and entered the roof. When they saw the alternate double of their ally Happy crying (though to Happy it was they who were the alternates), they softly placed their hands on Happy's shoulders in an effort to comfort him. "They're all..." Happy looked up at them, his eyes twinkling in the sunrise.

"Sanchii..." El Krunko II spit over the side of the wall, and since his aim was always dead-on-balls accurate, even when he wasn't actually aiming, it landed smack dab in the middle of Happy's puke pile. E.K II chugged his last beer, tossed that with perfect aim too, and burped as loud as he could. "Grand Emperor Gribulor made Sancho the Unstoppable Sanchez the second in command of his relentless imperial army of doom. They're nigh but unstoppable, and about 90% of the known galaxy has been flooded with their kind. That's why us resistance... Happy!?"

And Happy was off! He leapt across the rooftops as he made his way into the metropolis. Though his allies called his name, and he heard the sound of their footsteps chasing after him, they were no match for Happy's younger and more supple legs. After making a detour down a dark alley, Happy stopped a random passer-Sanchez, and ripped his head off. Sanchez blood gushed into the air, and Happy squealed with delight. He trotted down the lane, killing, ravaging, rampaging, and all around turning every fleshen thing he came across into hamburger. Within mere minutes he had turned all of downtown district C into chopped suey.

As he leaned against a bloodied street light to momentarily catch his breath, El Krunko II caught up to him, huffing and puffing.

"That won't... work... that'll... never work. You think we haven't... tried that before!!?"

Happy shrugged, and motioned around. "Are you kidding? That was great! Look at all this carnage! This is a good dent for a pre-breakfast assault if you ask me."

Ethnocentric Dracula II poofed into existence next to them both, huffing and puffing the same. After taking in the scene he slapped Happy across the face. "You moron. That never works."

Happy stood up, belligerent, and accosted the two of them. "You idiots never got anything right! That's why Gribulor's up there somewhere and you're down here. You think I'm gonna listen to you? Two losers? I must've wasted a *thousand* Sanchii already! How's *that* for not working?"

Thwoop! Pfwoop! Splish!

The trio looked up into the air.

"Behold..." El Krunko II muttered. "The re-population of the Sanchii."

A thousand tubes launched from the Sanchinator, and each vaporized high above the downtown district. Now, a thousand fully and individually dressed Sanchii were parachuting down into the city, fully prepared to continue the day where it had been so inconveniently chopped short.

"Quickly. Back here," E.D. II whispered. And the three of them disappeared into the back of an abandoned deli.

"And there's a fortress that rebuilds them just like that, on every single planet under Gribulor's malicious influence," El Krunko II explained, while exploring the abandoned icebox for abandoned beer.

This El Krunko sure has a drinking problem, Happy mused. *El Krunko would be pissed.* "Alright... So if I'm not able to take out the Sanchii directly... Then what's the *smart* play?"

El Krunko II miraculously revealed an iced over six pack. He sat down with it on the floor and grinned a toothy grin. "It is infinitely impossible for you to defeat your arch-nemesis in this time period," he said. "E.D. II is too old and feeble," E.D. II quacked in defiance, but El Krunko II continued. "And I've grown bored of killing Sanchii. It has dulled our desire for destruction and rid us of our resolve."

"Well what about *my* El Krunko, and *my* Ethnocentric Dracula?" Happy asked. "Can't we go through your portal thingamajig and rescue them?"

E.D. II had tears in his eyes, and Happy did not know why. El Krunko II cracked open one of the brewskies and crushed the whole thing before he finally answered. "I'm sorry Happy, but we can't. The destruction of the planet vaporized them into raw Higgs Bosons. They're gone."

"But you're time travelers!" Happy pointed out. "Can't we just go further back in time and save them?"

El Krunko II cracked open another beer, and after a long thoughtful pause, offered it to Happy. "No... They're gone... Forever." Happy reluctantly took the can and sighed with disbelief. E.K. II opened another for himself, and together they drank to their memories.

"Happy..." El Krunko II whispered. "There is only one thing left to do... You must venture forth into this time-line's Universe, to locate and bring back with you... The Epic of El Krunko."

TABLET: LXXXVII

"The Epic of El Krunko?" Happy repeated. "But..." He paused in thought and puzzled out the words. "But that's *your* name!" he finally cried out to El Krunko II.

"Indeed, for it is my Epic!" El Krunko II replied.

Happy was confused. "Where is it?" he asked.

"*That* is a secret lost to the ages!" El Krunko II answered in his best Epic voice.

Happy became angered by El Krunko II's vagueness about the whole Epic thing, and yelled out, "Then I shall go from one end of this galaxy to the next and find your ancient text! And you're comin' with me!" With that, he grabbed El Krunko II and E.D. II, and, using his powerful leg muscles, leapt into outer space. The force of his leap was so great the three found themselves hurtling through out of the atmosphere with ease and were soon off on a space-bound trajectory. El Krunko II, being the Lord of Slay II, was able to survive in the cold vacuum of space, but unfortunately E.D. II, the duck, could not. Yes. Even though he was a vampire.

When the trio finally collided with a planet, they did so, hard. Only Happy and El Krunko's great strength saved them from death, but E.D. II's already limp corpse exploded over Happy and El Krunko II.

When the dust settled and the pair arose, they realized with horror what had happened!

"Great Gribulor's Ghost!" Happy cried.

"Argh!" El Krunko II shouted.

Truly was this a dark day for the heroes.

Their ally was killed...

And they were all alone on an unknown planet!!

Dun Dun Dun!!

TABLET: LXXXVIII

The Dynamic Duo sat down upon the center of their large crater, and rested briefly (for the strain of interstellar leaps need not be mentioned here). As they lulled themselves into blissful rest, a huge sound disturbed their slumber. The ground all around them seemed to shake and vibrate, and the whole of the planet trembled.

"Happy!" A great voice boomed from the heavens. "El Krunko! I'm alive!"

"What the fuck?" the pair screamed and hopped to their feet.

"It is I. Ethnocentric Dracula. I used my Godly powers over matter and energy to reform myself, but I was totally vaporized! I seem to have become the entire planet itself, and I can't change back. Therefore Ethnocentric Dracula is no more. From here on I hereby proclaim myself to be... Planet Ethnocentric Dracula!" The planet shook and the skies cracked with thunder. "And hey! Check this out guys! Look what I can do!"

Where once it was day and a nearby star illuminated the skies with its light, the world was cast into darkness when Planet Ethnocentric Dracula took off, and flew his planet across the solar system. Nearby planets appeared at first as dots in the sky, and in mere seconds grew into their full planetary splendor. P.E.D. whipped past a few moons, and knocked them from their orbits. They careened down into the planet and a few seconds later, in an explosion that made each of heroes weep with joy, the planet and its moons were vaporized and turned to dust and rubble.

Happy Barrypants passed out from the shock.

El Krunko II leapt up and down in frabjously joyous excitement. "This is fucking awesome! With a planet for a space ship we can take over the whole fucking galaxy! Then, once we get our hands on my Epic, we'll travel back in time to before Gribulor took over, and lay that shit to waste, planet style!"

Planet Ethnocentric Dracula shook in agreement and said, "There appears to be a large civilization of pint sized bears on the other side of the ocean nearest you on the left facing the direction you are now."

EL Krunko II whipped out his version of the Ancestral Chainsaw and tossed the paralyzed Happy Barrypants on the back of his Intergalactic Ancestral Surfboard II. "Planet Ethnocentric Dracula!" he declared. "Head to the star system wherein can be found the Quest o' Matic 5000. Perhaps that piece of scrap metal could give you a Planet Quest which might lead us to the Epic."

"Aye aye Captain Krunko!" the planet spoke. And with that, El Krunko II was off surfing into the atmosphere while Planet Ethnocentric Dracula surfed through space.

TABLET: LXXXIX

Travel aboard the Surfboard of Surfing II was quick, and it was not long before El Krunko II entered bear territory. He proceeded to slay a great number of them, with the help of a few well timed earthquakes and volcanoes from Planet E.D. Eventually their leaders capitulated and declared El Krunko II King of all of Planet Ethnocentric Dracula. Satisfied with the title, he ruled justly and fairly over his bear subjects until they arrived at their destination, the solar system of the Quest o' Matic 5000.

It was not long before the task was done, and El Krunko II and Happy's paralyzed body found themselves near the very computer itself, for El Krunko II had traveled there to seek its wisdom before. The monstrous machine could be seen from miles away, atop a large hill around which was New New Silicon Valley.

El Krunko II surfed up to the Quest o' Matic 5000 and hopped off his surfboard. When he approached the great computer, its lights blinked and its gears whirled, and a printout came from a slot in its side. El Krunko II ripped the printout from the slot, held the paper close up to his aged eyes, and read it.

The printout, which reads:

"Greetings again El Krunko. It is good that you have come to seek me out once more. I have calculated the chances that you came here seeking the Epic of El Krunko to be 98.72354729237827%. And so, in the interest of expedience and efficiency, I will tell you this: it is stored within the memory cells of the long-dead Sing Potato that now dwells in the eye of Happy Barrypants, your companion. Come visit again soon. – Your inquiry has been processed and all fees have been charged to your account. The Quest o' Matic 5000 offers its advice on an 'as is' basis, without warranty, and is not liable for any loss or damage caused or alleged to be caused directly or indirectly by the information contained in this note. How did we do? Be sure to fill in a questionnaire on your way out. Thank you for visiting the Quest o' Matic 5000. Have a pleasant day. We hope to see you again for all your Questing needs. PS – Here's a tip! Present this note on your next visit and get a 5% discount. Offer expires in 1 standard year. Value: 1/100th of a cent."

El Krunko II returned to Planet Ethnocentric Dracula, lifted up the body of Happy, and spoke, "If you can, oh Sing Potato, speak with me now, and I would hear you recite the Epic of El Krunko!"

And indeed, the red hologram did appear, and it spoke loudly and clearly:

* * * * * * * * * *

The Epic of El Krunko

Bob the Martyr walked towards a town of Green Pig men. Upon his entrance, he was laughed at by all, for he was neither green nor a pig...

TABLET: XC

Langust, the Mayor of Green Pig town, arrived on the scene. He saw Bob the martyr and proclaimed him the new messiah. Upon this proclamation, the Green Pig Men fell to their knees and worshiped Bob.

TABLET: XCI

After a good hour of psalms and prayer, they hoisted the new found messiah upon high saying, "Bless this Bob, and he shall rule us Green Pig men from the walls of the mighty Cathedral." Thereupon they carried him into the Cathedral, wherein he was met with Cassandra the rotten, a leper who was their high priestess.

TABLET: XCII

Cassandra the leper proclaimed, "Bob is the messiah-martyr! Let this come to pass."

Bob was brought to a great pile of dynamite. "You will die for our cause," Cassandra declared. At that Bob was set on fire and tossed onto the great pyre of explosives. Ka-Boom!

The Mayor turned to Cassandra, who had lost an arm in the explosion. "What now?"

"To the battle-Porkin-Rorkin shuttle! The time has come for us to fight our war against the Purple Aardvarks of Go-Me-Shu."

TABLET: XCIII

Cassandra, who was a prophetess as well, said, "Your war against the Purple Aardvarks is doomed to fail... unless... you enlist the help of the Red Monkeys of Aamen-Kan."

Mayor Langust had no choice but to agree, and sent Mooshu the ambassador to petition the Red Moneys for military assistance.

TABLET: XCIV

Unfortunately, upon arrival at the village of the Red Monkeys of Aamen-Kan, Mooshu spied a great monkey dripping with ichor. Much to his dismay, he discovered the monkeys were meat-eaters, and their namesake came from them being red with blood.

Mooshu was captured, stuffed with apples, and roasted alive. Cassandra had foreseen this of course, as she was a prophetess, and she'd stuffed him previously with fireworks. When Mooshu was set upon the fire, her fireworks ignited and sent a glaring message into the sky.

Red Monkeys smell!
Sincerely,
Purple Aardvarks.

TABLET: XCV

Having gotten word of his brother Bob's demise, El Krunko, The Gimp Boy, left home to combat the Aardvarks, for it was a Tuesday, and he had nothing better to do. He grabbed the nearest celestial duck to the Aardvark world, and walked up to the high council. There sat the Spice Girls. El Krunko lifted his Guno-blasto-matic 2060 and offed all 8 of 'em!

TABLET: XCVI

After killing the Spice Girls, El Krunko came to the citadel of the Aardvark King Miguel Sanchez. Armed guards raced out to stop him. El Krunko smiled evilly, and whipped out his Ancestral Chainsaw. One by one he started slaying the aardvarks, cutting them up into little pieces while in his blood-soaked frenzy!

But alas! The true King of the Aardvarks, the Elephant Man, had hid himself behind the curtain, and raising his trunk on high, rushed forward, and gouged

El Krunko's eyes out with his tusks. El Krunko wandered out, blind and bleeding, while the Elephant Man took the Ancestral Chainsaw for his own, and rallied the remaining troops to storm the Green Pig men.

TABLET: XCVII

"Heba-Meba-Jeba-Cow!" El Krunko cried, and two new eyes appeared where his bloody eye sockets once were. He cried the words out again, and his Ancestral Chainsaw flew back into his hands, and in so doing removed the topmost portion of the elephants trunk, spouting blood and gore like a demented fountain. "By the power of Humbaba!" El Krunko declared, and at this the A.C. glowed crimson, in preparation to strike the evil Aardvarkian King. At this, El Krunko smote down the demon elephant King of Aardvarks and of evil and of all things wrong, down the center, cauterizing the wounds with its crimson blade.

TABLET: XCVIII

Upon killing the Elephant Man (who had a legitimate claim to the Aardvark throne, but held no official power and thus ruled behind the scenes), El Krunko busted into the palace chamber of Miguel Sanchez. Sanchez was not there, however, as he had left to oversee the attack on the Green Pig men. But had left behind his attractive bride, Pennsylvania Sanchez.

After having his way with her, El Krunko cast her aside, and boarded the largest star ship he could find to assist the Green Pigs in their war.

TABLET: XCIX

Unfortunately, since star ship fuel had not been invented yet (as the inventor of the ship was temporally challenged, and created things backwards), it crashed, and was broken. In the ensuing explosion, El Krunko was very badly burned. While crawling from the wreck his eyes were melted away by burning sulfur. He escaped the wreckage and wandered blindly towards the village.

Meanwhile, Miguel Sanchez had ordered the Goblins (code for Green Organic Blower-uppers), to cut wood make a mighty war machine capable of breaking down the defensive walls that they might storm the village.

But on the horizon... there was a hint of red....

TABLET: C

Annoyed at the ever painful plot twist, El Krunko again bellowed out, "Heba-Meba-Jeba-cow," and his eyes returned once more. With the ability to see he located battle-Porkin-Rorkin shuttle which *did* have fuel, and made his way to Carlos V.

TABLET: CI

El Krunko arrived just in time to see Miguel Sanchez's forces storm the Green Pig city. Knowing immediately that the battle was hopeless unless he did something drastic, El Krunko leapt into the Lake of Power and grew fangs. Encouraged by his new power, El Krunko leapt again, only this time into the fray, and started searching for his childhood sweetheart, the

Green Pig Brunhilda.

TABLET: CII

And so, El Krunko pushed on, slaying Aardvarks left and right in the dark of night with his newly grown fangs. After a great journey across the Poker Flats, he reached the luminous Cave of Souls. It was there that he'd hope to find his love Brunhilda.

Deep in the bowels of the cave he came to an empty chamber. El Krunko spoke the magic words, "Mecha Lom Di Laurence Olivier!" and the wall slid open. There she was… Brunhilda, as beautiful as ever. He took some magic dust from his pouch, and scattered it in the air, calling out, "Come to me!" and some other magic jazz. The bones rattled, and his necromantic skills were complete. To give the corpse true life, he cut his eyes from his head, and placed them in hers. When the blood spewed forth, she rose.

TABLET: CIII

El Krunko woke up from his dream with a fright. He had grown so tired from the slaughter that he'd fallen asleep in the blood of his enemies. His encounter with Brunhilda had only been a dream. After a great big yawn, El Krunko stood, and entered the Green Pig town.

TABLET: CIV

El Krunko asked everyone he met about his lost lover, (and what a passionate lover indeed!) but it was all to no avail, and he could not find her. Furious with his ill fortune, he whipped out the A.C. and killed the nearest citizen. Guards who witnessed the spectacle immediately rushed up and seized the blood thirsty, stupefied hero figure.

He was tried, convicted, and sentenced to the same fate as his martyr brother.

TABLET: CV

The war against the Purple Aardvarks had ended with victory for the Green Pigs. But Miguel Sanchez' body had not been found, and some believed he'd returned to his planet unscathed.

And indeed it was true, for once Miguel Sanchez returned home, his wife Pennsylvania told him of how El Krunko had ravished her. Furious, Miguel Sanchez sent a telegram to the Green Pig planet and challenged El Krunko to combat. The Green Pigs, being honorable (and also lazy), agreed for El Krunko to meet Miguel Sanchez and battle him, mano a mano.

Langust, the Mayor of El Krunko's town, agreed that this would be El Krunko's trial for any crimes which had been caused by him over the course of the war.

TABLET: CVI

The two of them met at high noon. It was raining, and the town was silent. Hundreds of Green Pigs stood on the four sides of the square. Miguel Sanchez and El Krunko stepped forward. "Choose your weapons!" El Krunko chose his Ancestral Chainsaw, while Miguel Sanchez picked out a chrome .357 Magnum. They placed their backs together, marched ten paces, and waited for the bell sounded noon. But no shots rang out when the time arrived.

Miguel Sanchez vanished! It was a hologram trap! Thousands of battle ready Aardvark paratroopers started falling from the sky!

TABLET: CVII

The battle that ensued lasted many days (with short breaks for tea and crumpets promptly at 3 o'clock), and was characterized with the sounds of numerous pig squeals, chainsaw roars from the A.C., and that noise that aardvarks make. 40 days and 40 nights later, El Krunko stood triumphantly amongst 1000's upon 1000's of dead Aardvarks and Green Pigs alike. All that remained of the Green Pig race were two males, the Mayor Langust, and a lowly fledgling pig named Grunta-Grunta-Pow-Wow.

Indignant, Langust screamed out, "It is a good day to die! ... FOR AARDVARKS!"

Grunta-Grunta-Pow-Wow replied, "I Hate those Muther-Fuckin-kunt-drippin-small-peenied cock whore bitches from my ass!" (For he was foul mouthed.)

TABLET: CVIII

El Krunko agreed with Grunta-Grunta-Pow-Wow and Langust's sentiments, but he was forced to explain that their war would never truly end until Miguel Sanchez was dead.

Unfortunately, as every schoolboy knows that Miguel Sanchez cannot be defeated by normal means alone, they needed to come up some kind of plan.

El Krunko left Langust and Grunta-Grunta-

Pow-Wow behind to rebuild the Green Pig civilization, and traveled alone to the planet of Og. There, El Krunko visited Dr. Elvis Frankenstein, the brilliant but twisted geneticist who made money grow on trees, and had invented both the peanut, and pro-wrestling.

TABLET: CIX

El Krunko knocked at the doctor's door, and even went so far as to ring the door bell when knocking didn't quite cut it, but he would not receive an answer. Enraged, El Krunko whipped out his A.C. and tore the door down. Once inside, he discovered why he'd been ignored.

In a horrible experiment gone wrong, Dr. Elvis Frankenstein, the brilliant but twisted geneticist, had accidentally transferred his intellectual genius into the mind of a chicken, and the chicken mind into his. Elvis's human body, clucking around, had activated a 9 Megahertz computer, and the brilliant but twisted mind of Elvis Frankenstein was blown apart in a horrible twist of fate.

El Krunko did not give up, however, for there was a great chest filled with gravy and directions. One of which could enhance his Ancestral Chainsaw with an upgrade capable of hurting Miguel Sanchez. But he still needed the Elusive Black Potato.

"This fools a cluck," Langust declared.

"Fucking Chicken!" replied Grunta-Grunta-Pow-Wow, at a loss for a better insult.

(Let it be known that the skulls of the common chicken [Chickenus Cluckus Normalus] are extremely vulnerable to the energy emitted by 9 Megahertz computers, as it is at that precise frequency where the brain cavity vibrates uncontrollably until the inevitable outcome: exploding everywhere. This can be easily substantiated with a plethora of scientific study, but for best results, find a 9 Megahertz computer, and get yourself a chicken.)

El Krunko, thoroughly disheartened with the task of locating the E.B.P., decided it would be best to instead wander the vastness of space for a while until something interesting happened.

TABLET: CX

7 years and a cool goatee later…

TABLET: CXI

El Krunko arrived on the planet Ufgor and finally found the elusive black potato. Now with it in his possession, El Krunko knew he finally had what it would take to overthrow the evil dictator Miguel Sanchez.

And so, El Krunko and his trusty companions Langust and Grunta-Grunta-Pow-Wow (who had stowed away on El Krunko's ship 7 years earlier after realizing that they, in fact, could not rebuild the Green Pig civilization), went to Go-me-shu to confront Miguel Sanchez once and for all. Since El Krunko demanded that his final confrontation be mano a mano, as he was once promised, Langust and Grunta-Grunta-Pow-Wow were left to roam the countryside in search of El Krunko's love Brunhilda, the only female Green Pig left in the Universe.

TABLET: CXII

When El Krunko crested the hill which overlooked Miguel Sanchez's home citadel, he was shocked to find instead a barren wasteland. His mighty fortress and the surrounding Purple Aardvark civilization were completely gone. He scoured the remains of the once great city for clues, but found not a single lead. Depressed at the dead end, El Krunko returned to the rendezvous point and met with Grunta-Grunta-Pow-Wow and Langust, who were equally unsuccessful.

El Krunko and his allies, too tired to consider their next move, retired to their space ship, and launched into orbit for a fancy meal that Grunta-Grunta-Pow-Wow had so graciously prepared.

After devouring the feast, El Krunko asked, "Tell me... What is this, and where did you get this food?"

Grunta-Grunta-Pow-Wow smiled at the shout out to the chef. "It's fucking potato pancakes, that's what it is. I found some gravy and a big black potato in a crate in the back."

"No! You Fool! You cooked our last hope against Miguel Sanchez." Taken by his rage, El Krunko leapt upon the table ready to throttle Grunta-Grunta-Pow-Wow with his bare hands, but landed on an olive fork, and lost his eyes in the process.

TABLET: CXIII

Further enraged, El Krunko whipped out the old trusty Ancestral Chainsaw and slashed about in blind hysterics. Before he had finally managed to calm himself, he had taken the arms off Langust, a leg from Grunta-Grunta-Pow-Wow, and turned the battle-Porkin-Rorkin shuttle into battle-Porkin-Rorkin scrap metal.

"Heba-Meba-Jeba-Cow!" Pop! Pop! El Krunko had his eyes again. When he saw the mess he had made, El Krunko became so perplexed as to what he should do now, that he began to cry. Langust and Grunta-Grunta-Pow-Wow tended to their wounds (though they remained limbless).

TABLET: CXIV

Depressed at his failure, El Krunko shot himself out the airlock. As he floated aimlessly through space, El Krunko spied a Purple Aardvark shuttle, and managed to gran onto its bumper. The ship flew for a few days, and in order to survive El Krunko was forced to eat his own appendix.

When the shuttle finally landed on Melph-Kelph-Lelph-Pelph-Zelph, El Krunko discovered that the Purple Aardvarks had simply moved their civilization, or at the very least, colonized the place. He questioned the first passing aardvark, who gave him the response, "There was so much pollution on Go-Me-Shu, that people began to spontaneously combust, so we moved here."

TABLET: CXV

Extraordinarily enraged (even for El Krunko), at the thought that the Purple Aardvarks would be so anti-nature enough to pollute their world only to abandon it, he whipped out his Ancestral Chainsaw and slew the aardvark right then and there. Dragging its body behind a tool shed, he skinned it, and wore its skin on over his. Now looking like the enemy, El Krunko passed unquestioned into the innermost levels of Miguel Sanchez's not-so-secret citadel. While traversing the corridor he found a room marked, "Do not enter! Emperor's private chamber!" El Krunko's eyes twitched as he got a bright idea.

He dimmed the lights in the hall, and made a small slit in his pelt so it looked like he was wounded. After he prepared himself for the role of a lifetime with a deep breath, El Krunko pulled the fire alarm and pounded on the door in a huff. Guards were quickly on the scene.

"Help! An intruder broke out of Miguel Sanchez's quarters and escaped that way!" he told the guards. "Open the door so I can see if anything's missing!"

Either the guards were dumb, or his acting was incredible, for they fell for his trap.

TABLET: CXVI

El Krunko burst into Miguel Sanchez' private chambers, where he was found with his pants down and a copy of Play-aardvark to the side. "Who let you in here – OH MY GOD IT'S EL KRUNKO!!!!"

El Krunko whipped out the A.C. and Miguel Sanchez got out his Gumppnarish velvita. The battle that followed was grisly, for Miguel Sanchez had not pulled up his pants, and was soon made a eunuch by El Krunko's means.

TABLET: CXVII

"You fool!" Miguel Sanchez cried. "Don't you realize you cannot defeat me without the black potato! Ha, ha ha!"

Whether his encounter with the lake of power was a dream or not, El Krunko did not know, but in that moment magic fangs appeared in his mouth, and he felt overcome with even more bloodlust than usual. He tossed the Ancestral Chainsaw aside and sunk his fangs into Miguel Sanchez neck. Miguel Sanchez cried out in pain and fear as the blood drained from his body, and he soon fell to the ground, dead.

El Krunko screamed in victory, and when Pennsylvania Sanchez entered to see what the fuss was all about, El Krunko had his way with her, again.

TABLET: CXVIII

After many hours of having his way, El Krunko grew tired, and fell asleep. Pennsylvania rose quietly, her plan falling into place, and took the A.C. from where it lay near Miguel Sanchez's mutilated body. She took the blood from it, and snuck from the room. Hours later, El Krunko awoke to find both his woman and his weapon gone. Enraged, he leapt from the bed, and trailed the blood spots that she'd left behind, for the blood was much (El Krunko never really, actually *drank* it), and it had soaked her shoes. The trail led through a dark secret passageway and emerged in a hidden room deep beneath the fortress. He moved in quietly, pushed open the door, and dropped to his knees in horror. The cloning chambers of Miguel Sanchez! Egad no!

TABLET: CXIX

To his far left stood Pennsylvania Sanchez, while to his far right his sacred Ancestral Chainsaw with karate chopping action was sitting on a pedestal. El Krunko made his choice, and lunged for his trusty old A.C. Pennsylvania pushed the button she had been discreetly hiding. She bellowed forth, "Petty man! Slayer of my love and taker of my body... Now face the relentless Sanchez army of DOOM!" A hiss of steam released from the rising central doorway, and an uncountable number of Miguel Sanchii poured forth into the room.

The Sanchii, in unison: "We are as numerous as the sands on the beach, and the stars in the sky."

TABLET: CXX

El Krunko cried out in terror. He revved up his Ancestral Chainsaw and started hacking away at the clones. But it was hopeless. And when the time came that El Krunko was just about to succumb to the unstoppable hordes, Grunta-Grunta-Pow-Wow and Langust burst in, the latter carrying a double barrel shotgun, and both with freshly replaced robotic limbs. They leapt into the fray and began to slay Miguel Sanchii with the same zest and vigor as El Krunko.

TABLET: CXXI

They quickly discovered, however, that even though they were taking out Miguel Sanchii left and right, each time one would meet its end, 4 new ones would step from the chambers to replace their fallen comrade. "Flee friends! Flee! The Miguel Sanchii are too many!" El Krunko roared. Langust whammed and boomed the shotgun and they made their way towards the door, but to their misfortune it had been locked behind them by one of the Sanchii!

"Our end is upon us," El Krunko said sadly. "Farewell Grunta-Grunta-Pow-Wow! Goodbye Langust! Eeep!" Just as the inevitably fatal blow was about to befall El Krunko, the wall crashed down, and Elvis the Chicken Frankenstein, who had tarred and feathered himself for clothing, burst into the cloning chamber with a sledgehammer and a Gatling gun. Huzzah! The chicken strikes back!

TABLET: CXXII

El Krunko leapt to the side of his ally, Elvis the Chicken, and the Miguel Sanchii balked in simultaneous horror at the sight of the Dynamic Duo. "Grunta-Grunta-Pow-Wow! Langust!" El Krunko cried out. "Stand your ground!"

While frozen in fear, the horde of Sanchii continued to multiply, and soon had grown to astronomical proportions. Sanchii flowed forth from the vile place, flying off the planet and into the far reaches of the galaxy, by means which cannot be known. The group, determined to stop the insidious threat, charged forward to carve out their piece of the Relentless Sanchii Army of Doom.

TABLET: CXXIII

After 40 days and 40 nights of battle, El Krunko and his allies had finally rid Melph-Kelph-Lelph-Phelp-

Zelph of every last one of the Miguel Sanchii. A necessary part of the process was the destruction of the cloning chambers. Pennsylvania Sanchez begged El Krunko for mercy, and he gave it only after having his way with her for yet another 40 days and 40 nights. As he had rid the planet of the tyrannical Miguel Sanchez, El Krunko became the King of the Purple Aardvarks, and married Pennsylvania. Thusly, she changed her name to Pennsylvania Krunko.

TABLET: CXXIV

King El Krunko was the newly proclaimed, "Master of the Universe." In one ultimate decree to the aardvarkian folk, he commanded them all to kill themselves in atonement for prior evils against the Red Monkeys and Green Pigs. And so they did, and the aardvarks of the colour purple were no more.

"Fuckin' aardvarks! Go to hell!" yelped Grunta-Grunta-Pow-Wow.

King El Krunko looked out over the remaining population of his kingdom, which consisted of his wife and three sidekicks. "A new day is dawning citizens..." their King told them. "And we all shall be the leaders of the new order."

"Of what you big fat walking fuck?" screamed Grunta-Grunta-Pow-Wow. "You killed all of your subjects you fucking ASSHOLE!" he screamed again.

King El Krunko sighed. "You've always been a thorn in my side, Grunta-Grunta-Pow-Wow."

TABLET: CXXV

Upon declaring his distaste for the pig, King El

Krunko whipped out his A.C. and carved Grunta-Grunta-Pow-Wow into little itty bits of bacon, and offered him roasted and seasoned to the remainder of the citizens. King El Krunko and Langust declined, for they were no cannibals, but Pennsylvania and Elvis the Chicken joined in on the feast.

It was not long before King El Krunko had become bored with ruling over a species that no longer existed, so he tossed his style of King aside, and resolved to leave the planet in search for new adventures, after all, there were still Miguel Sanchii freely roaming the Universe, though El Krunko knew there were too many to bother tracking down. While Pennsylvania and Langust were packing their bags, and El Krunko was taking one last look around the place, Mecha-Godzilla attacked the palace.

TABLET: CXXVI

"Oh no! It's Mecha-Godzilla!" El Krunko cried.

Pennsylvania ran out to the terrace to join her husband. "Come! Follow me! We can seek shelter in the castle basement!"

The two of them climbed down the fire escape, and Langust followed after. Once safe, they turned on the security monitors and accessed the outside feed. El Krunko was aghast, and Pennsylvania wept. Mecha-Godzilla had destroyed their castle, and was now making short work of their ship.

Just then, a great wave of wind and dust knocked out the cameras. Their screens went black, and they huddled together in the pitch dark of the basement. Outside a new roar was heard beyond just the tyrannical roar of Mecha-Godzilla's speakers. Then came the large booms, and the roaring, and screeching, and finally... silence. They climbed up through the rubble, and found the battered and broken remains of an organic Mecha-Godzilla-like creature. Lakes of blood pooled round the enormous corpse.

Pennsylvania, who had a PhD in forensic science, analyzed the blood, and finally declared, "Mecha-Godzilla, beat Godzilla to death."

TABLET: CXXVII

Langust was at the end of his rope. "Well... Well that's, that's just great, man. What... I mean what are we goin' to do now? This Godzilla machine will get us <u>all</u> man! That's it man! It's game over man! Game over!"

TABLET: CXXVIII

El Krunko slapped Langust across the face. "Pull yourself together! We need to work together if we're ever to defeat Mecha-Godzilla and get out of here!"

As if on cue, Mecha-Godzilla appeared behind them. El Krunko drew his A.C. and Langust loaded his shotgun. Pennsylvania, not knowing what to do, hurled small rocks at the monstrous metal beast. "Attack!" El Krunko cried, and he and Langust engaged the giant robot in Mortal Kombat, an arcade machine which had suddenly fallen from the sky.

TABLET: CXXIX

They fought for what seemed like an eternity. Elvis the Chicken, who had returned from vacation, constantly traded in singles for quarters at the local automated bank. In the end, however, both Langust and El Krunko were no match for Mecha-Godzilla. He, being a machine, knew all the moves, and even a few fatalities. Once, just once however, he did perform a friendship. This one time made Pennsylvania happy, and she challenged Mecha-Godzilla, thinking it had a good side. They played, and oddly enough, perhaps through sheer luck, or even through divine intervention, Pennsylvania won. Enraged, Mecha-Godzilla bent down, and ate them all in one heaving gulp.

TABLET: CXXX

Inside the beast, the Triumphant Trio (and Elvis), found the controls to Mecha-Godzilla on auto pilot, set to destroy. El Krunko killed the auto pilot and grabbed the controls.

"Score," proclaimed El Krunko, and he flew Mecha-Godzilla to the deep reaches of space.

TABLET: CXXXI

The Triumphant Trio (and Elvis), flew to the planet of Morgun-Boo. Upon the planet there lived a race of large, shoe-like men called the Syro-Lebs. The Syro-Lebs saw Mecha-Godzilla land on their planet, and were frightened.

TABLET: CXXXII

Perhaps it was spontaneous hysteria that formed within his mind due to the malignant little toe tumor destined to be his undoing. Or perhaps it was because he was bored. Either way, El Krunko strapped his seat belt on. "Alright everybody, strap in. Papa needs a new home planet!" With an evil grin, El Krunko flipped the controls to destroy, ultra-style.

TABLET: CXXXIII

A terrifying screech bellowed out from the mechanical beast. All the retarded little shoe-like men were hit by a cannibalizer ray, and started biting one another. In time only one Syro-Leb remained, plump from consuming all the other Syro-Lebi of the planet. Mecha-Godzilla ate the Oyster of the Sea (for that was its name), and threw him up in chunks shortly thereafter.

TABLET: CXXXIV

"Excellent!" El Krunko proudly exclaimed, but all that automatic slaughter had made him sleepy. He parked Mecha-Godzilla at the edge of the woods, set it for night-mode, and took a nap.

Meanwhile, the remainder of the Triumphant Trio (and Elvis), exited Mecha-Godzilla, eager to explore the forest. It was not long before they stumbled across the Cave of Souls (it was labeled as such), and entered. They were immediately assaulted with images of the spirits of the dead.

Langust was accosted by the ghost of Grunta-Grunta-Pow-Wow, Pennsylvania by the ghost of Miguel Sanchez, and Elvis the Chicken Frankenstein by the soul of the true Dr. Elvis Frankenstein. All three were driven stark-raving mad, and left the cave foaming at the mouth.

TABLET: CXXXV

When El Krunko woke up he was alone. He gathered his things and followed in the footsteps of his companions, eventually making his way to the Cave of Souls. El Krunko had his destiny before him. He'd dreamed of this moment where he would see his Brunhilda again. In his dreams he somehow knew this, all of this, was but the first step to inherit the Universe. "Mecha Lom Di Laurence Olivier!" The passage opened before him. He stepped through, proud of his ingeniousness, and just as he was expecting to see Brunhilda's dead body, he gasped one final gasp, and fell to the ground, paralyzed.

"Excellent shot, oh lord! Quite splendid, yes, yes. Quite splendid indeed!" A short Englishman looked up at Quito Von Libinschtein, the inventor of Mecha-Godzilla.

"Vell, vell, vell. El Krunko. Ve shall see who has ze advantage now!"

TABLET: CXXXVI

Quito Von Libinschtein disappeared into the darkness of the cave... only to reappear moments later, racing towards a paralyzed El Krunko in a silver BMW.

TABLET: CXXXVII

El Krunko laughed, for he had long since become immune to paralysis potions (it's the first thing any good King does), and when he rose he whipped out his Ancestral Chainsaw and carved the silver BMW in two. But as he did so, the engine block exploded, and both he and Quito Von Libinschtein were consumed in flames.

"Argh!" the German inventor screamed, as he stopped, dropped, and rolled. El Krunko, (who was impervious to fire), laughed again, much louder, when suddenly Quito Von Libinschtein's tiny English assistant, Lord Byron Powers, engaged him in combat with an Ancestral Leafblower.

TABLET: CXXXVIII

"You have severely burned my master!" Byron shouted. "Meet your doom!" He revved up his Ancestral Leafblower and blew hot acid everywhere. Laughing maniacally, Lord Byron Powers walked steadily towards El Krunko.

"Alright, El Krunko, you've got this!" El Krunko yelled, "Just remember that song! You know this. You know this!" He clenched his fist and closed his eyes to concentrate. "Something, something, you will see, you'll avoid catastrophe!" Annoyed that he was short on memory, El Krunko cleaved Lord Byron Powers and his A.L. in twain. "And that, as they say, is that."

But when he turned to slay Quito Von Libinschtein, the man was gone.

TABLET: CXXXIX

El Krunko, with trusty A.C. in hand, rushed down the only apparent tunnel that Quito Von Libinschtein could escape through. At the end a great door impeded his further pursuit. "This looks like a job for... the Ancestral Chainsaw!" After 5 minutes of mad hacking, El Krunko dashed into the room, only to see the healed German fascist slide into his newest diabolical creation.

Truck-a-saurus-Rex!

TABLET: CXL

"Good God!" El Krunko cried. "Sweet Mary and Joseph! Jesus H. Christ!" El Krunko was shocked and stupefied. Quito Von Libinschtein revved up the Truck-a-saurus-Rex and lumbered towards him. El Krunko chopped at the dinosaurian automobile with his A.C., but it was to no avail!

Quito Von Libinschtein laughed maniacally. "El Krunko, you fool. Don't you know that your name is merely Spanish for, 'The Krunko!' "

El Krunko moaned in sorrow, and the fascist ran him over.

TABLET: CXLI

Quito Von Libinschtein screamed in ecstasy. "Ah ha! Mein friend the Krunko. I have slain thee. I will rule all!" Thinking that the pool of blood trickling out from beneath Truck-a-saurus-Rex's treads was El Krunko's dead bile, Von Libinschtein leapt down from his control platform, exited his robotic monstrosity, and entered his Cryonics Chamber. He took from it a great red vial, and a horde of green and brown masses, and set to work on them at the table.

El Krunko rejoiced. Though short of breath, he had been pushed down into the ground unseen. When the time was ripe, El Krunko pushed a secret button on his collar. Moments later Mecha-Godzilla ripped the roof off, and smashed its hand into the floor.

El Krunko spoke into his collar. "Mecha-Godzilla, destroy his lab." And so the gigantic robot obeyed, and it began by first wrecking the table, and its chemical supply.

"Ach! No! Mein Lunch!" Quito Von Libinschtein cried out. "Ach, and mein evil creation! No!"

TABLET: CXLII

Fire bellowed forth from Mecha-Godzilla's maw, and the entire place was set ablaze. But the mad invented would not be so easily defeated, and when Quito Von Libinschtein hopped into the far superior Truck-a-saurus-Rex, he quickly destroyed Mecha-Godzilla.

"Ach! Truck-a-saurus-Rex beeeeeeat Mecha-Godzilla to his demise." Libinschtein cackled. "Ahh ahhahaha."

El Krunko sobbed like a baby, because he lost to the bad guy, big time.

He had truly fallen from grace.

TABLET: CXLIII

Quito Von Libinschtein chuckled heartily at El Krunko's sorrow. With even his moral victory won, off he drove in Truck-a-saurus-Rex, away from the burning facility and into the woods, leaving El Krunko to himself. Our hero eventually composed himself enough to recover his fallen weapon, and approach the fallen remains of Mecha-Godzilla. "Scrap metal to scrap metal, rust to rust..." he said, and with that, buried the faithful robot. He was about to burst into tears again, when he saw a light sparkling in the far distance of the cave.

TABLET: CXLIV

Interested in the shiny, El Krunko raced to the end of the cave and discovered a great find: Dr. Quito Von Libinschtein's monocle! "What is this?" he bellowed out in standard Krunko-speak. He picked up the monocle, and peered through it. This was all it took to set it off. The Great Monocle of Genius was responsible for inspiring the Dr. to create Truck-a-saurus-Rex and Mecha-Godzilla, and as of that moment became permanently affixed to El Krunko's head.

"By Job, I do believe I'm a smart man." He

quietly rejoiced the fortuitous turn of events, and set to work on Dr. El Krunko's (his PhD came from a nearby vending Machine), new warrior army.

It consisted of Mecha-Rodan, Mecha-Monster 0, and Mecha-Mothra.

TABLET: CXLV

But his work was cut short, and his creations remained unfinished, for Truck-a-saurus-Rex burst into Dr. El Krunko's lab. In his zainy German accent, Quito Von Libinschtein spurted out, "Uh-huhu-robotic dinosaurs are cool. Huh huh." For the bad doctor's intelligence had finally drained away, and he had been reduced to an idiot without his monocle, as a result of his dependency on the precious artifact for so many years of inventing.

With one great thump of the robot's fist he

crushed Dr. El Krunko, and the monocle as well, and wandered off into the forest smashing stuff (because it was cool).

Quito Von Libinschtein had fallen from grace too.

TABLET: CXLVI

Dr. El Krunko was busy wondering if, without his monocle, they'd take his PhD away from him, when suddenly, the board of directors of the American Chemical Society, presided over by Mustard Wigbottom, entered Dr. El Krunko's lab, and ripped his doctorate from his hands.

In that horrifying spectacle, Dr. El Krunko was no more, and he was reduced to the mundane, and inferior, Mr. El Krunko.

Truly, he had fallen from grace.

After the board of directors fled the scene, Mr. El Krunko resolved to travel even further into the cave in search of Brunhilda, and more adventures.

TABLET: CXLVII

Reduced to merely Mr. El Krunko, he ventured to the deepest sections of Quito Von Libinschtein's former laboratory. Breaking open the barred walls, he strode fearlessly into the darkness. Mr. El Krunko found that somehow the chemical gasses there which leaked from the bowels of the earth, gave him the ability to spontaneously combust at will. Lighting the way with his pinky (for it would not be missed), he passed the metaphorical barrier into the underworld, passed the spirits of the A.A. helpers, passed the audience of

Geraldo, and passed even the creator of Barney. Yes, Mr. El Krunko was descending into Hell.

TABLET: CXLVIII

"Ah, the Realm of Hades. Quite comfy if I do say so myself," proclaimed El Krunko (for he had decided it would be best to conceal his identity as a Mr. lest that be taken from his as well, and he be reduced to no formal style whatsoever.)

Satan walked up to El Krunko and declared, in a Mexican accent, "Ey meng. Que Pasa? Seems you've fallen from grace, esse. You can chill with me and be evil and stuff, holmes.

"Cool!" replied El Krunko. Fully fallen from grace, and in the presence of the Dark Lord, El Krunko decided that his campaign of evil and destruction had finally begun.

TABLET: CXLIX

Now that El Krunko was evil, he needed to do evil things, but was unaccustomed to the alignment, and felt unsure of how to proceed. At long last he sought advice from Satan, who was busy whipping a damned soul while betting on the results of a soap opera.

"Well, my good lad, since you are a beginner," Satan said in his wormy English way, "why don't you start with some good old fashioned pillaging."

Thusly, El Krunko traveled to the city of Bob, where many humans lived. Once there he began his assigned duties, when out of nowhere the heroic Captain Northwestern Hemisphere (C.N.H.) appeared, and punched El Krunko's lights out.

TABLET: CL

El Krunko awoke to find himself in a dark room. He sat up from the un-comfy cushion and opened the door, only to find himself back in Hell!

"Egads!!" El Krunko yelped, "Nos foratum in lama mana," for he now spoke Latin.

Wandering the land of the dead, and thoroughly depressed that C.N.H. had killed him, El Krunko decided it best to trick Satan into bringing him back to life.

(Subtitled) "Satan. May I walk your dog?"

"Yo chiero Cerebus," Satan bellowed out in broken Central American. "Give him a good shit." And so, after Satan turned back to playing Mortal Kombat with the dead soul of Mecha-Godzilla, El Krunko took his dog Cerebus out for a walk. And with his new faithful hound in tow, pledged vengeance on Captain Northwestern Hemisphere.

TABLET: CLI

Once back at the city of Bob, El Krunko the Evil found Captain Northwestern Hemisphere cleaning up the pillaging. El Krunko the Evil told the Chico-Cerebus, "Sic em boys!" Without hesitation, the doggies devoured Captain Northwestern Hemisphere, who screamed in agony as he was exposed to vile bile and other digestive juices.

Upon C.N.H.'s death, a great rift in the earth broke open, and Satan appeared to confront El Krunko. The Dark Lord lumbered forward, preparing to kill El Krunko, and return him to hell where he couldn't cause any more mischief in the land of the living.

TABLET: CLII

El Krunko revved up his Ancestral Chainsaw and tried to make short work of Satan, but his mighty weapon had no effect on the Dark Lord. Satan laughed heartily and chewed on his hay. "El Krunko, you must know that you can only defeat me by answering this riddle: Why is a raven like a writing desk?"

El Krunko sat in contemplation for 40 days and 40 nights, before he finally proclaimed, "Because they both begin with R."

Satan chuckled. "Fine. Stay here if you want." And with that, the Dark Lord retrieved Cerebus by his chain, and disappeared, leaving the now less-evil El Krunko alone in the abandoned city of Bob.

TABLET: CLIII

The people in Bob were once all stubby and stout, but were also renowned for their trucks. El Krunko walked over to the nearest vending machine, inserted 5,000,000,000 Kerbanbal ($5 American), and out flew a truck. A truck as strong as two two trucks. A truck that could move faster than four trucks. El Krunko adopted it as his son. So was born, "El Trucko."

TABLET: CLIV

El Krunko hopped in El Trucko's driving seat and punched it into overdrive. He tore up the streets and exited the town (hitting two Miguel Sanchii who had wandered into Bob on the way.) He drove straight across space and time, and returned to Cave of Souls, where he parked El Trucko and entered. After a brief meal, he began again to look for signs of Brunhilda, when he accidentally stumbled upon the lost civilization of Ugh-bug. The members of this tribal society captured El Krunko, and threw him into a pot of boiling water.

"That'll be good eating," the King of Ugh-bug declared to his subjects.

As the Ugh-bugs cheered the soon-to-be boiled El Krunko on, our hero desperately tried to figure a way out. He could not see anything in the cauldron, for inside was a dark, viscous, green, pea-soup-like soup, and the dismembered hands they'd added for flavor really grossed him out.

El Krunko closed his eyes, and remembered back to a time when he was Pequerto Krunko, and thought of how he used to make messes in the bathroom. He remembered how he used to make waves by rocking back and forth. He replicated the technique in the cauldron, and the pot began a-rockin. Before long he'd managed to knock the cauldron over, sending a wave of very-warm soup flying at the crowd of Ugh-bugs.

TABLET: CLV

The Ugh-Bugs struck by the soup screamed out in pain. "We're melting! Melting!" Plumes of smoke rose from their corpses.

Soon El Krunko stood alone amidst a sea of melted Ugh-bug gore. All around him were the remains of his accidental genocide. "Eh..." He shrugged.

When from the sky, 5 beams of rainbow light transported Dr. Quito Von Libinschtein and 4 Miguel Sanchii to the surface of the planet. They appeared before him clothed in uniquely colored rainbow spandex with snazzy helmets. Quito Von Libinschtein yelled out, in his zainy German accent, "It's morphine, I mean morphing time!" Gibberish followed. It contained really long names of dinosaurs, occasionally followed by the word, "Power!" spoke in unison by the team.

TABLET: CLVI

When from the sky fell several gigantic metal dinosaurs. Alas, as the robotic monstrosities hit the ground they shattered into pieces. "Aye carumba!" cried the newly monocled Quito Von Libinschtein. "On to plan B!" He and the Miguel Sanchii shrieked out the names of various Shakespearean characters, and as if by some magic or advanced technology, none other than the characters-made-flesh of Hamlet, Othello, Macbeth, and Julius Caesar appeared at their sides, ready for combat.

"To be or not to be? That is the question!" Hamlet declared, and with that raced towards El Krunko, rapier in hand. El Krunko looked around desperately, but his A.C. was nowhere in sight!

TABLET: CLVII

Not knowing what to do, El Krunko mad a hasty retreat and fled into a nearby forest. Beneath the canopy of leaves the forest turned as dark as night, and there, in the shadows, he saw something glimmering. El Krunko soon discovered that the light was but the shimmering of a familiar sword from his childhood. He held the aged weapon aloft and declared, "By the power of Greyskull, I am... ok... El Krunko?"

But no special fx followed. Instead, a voice from the darkness replied, "You fool. Only *I* can say that!" And out stepped He-Man: Master of the Universe, with Optimus Prime: Leader of the Autobots, and Liono: Lord of the Thundercats, with She-ra: Princess of Power.

"Wow!" El Krunko was star-struck, "I love all your shows!"

Soon, El Krunko and his band of eighties-cartoon-hero team leaders prepared for battle with the squad of scholarly Shakespearians.

TABLET: CLVIII

The Shakespearians drew their rapiers, blasters, and wits, and drew forward to battle saying things like, "Et tu, will DIE!" and, "The taste of my sharp wit alone will slay thee, no less my sword!" and, "Piss off there Bruce."

The eighties-cartoon-heroes all rushed into battle flailing their arms like idiots.

Shakespeare's men were killed instantly.

Unfortunately for the fearsome group, Shakespeare himself had appeared to do battle.

TABLET: CLIX

Angered that his characters were so easily killed, Shakespeare unsheathed his razor-sharp wit and slit the throats of He-Man, Optimus Prime, Liono, and She-ra without a second thought. When he moved to do the same to El Krunko, however, El Krunko ducked, and Shakespeare's wit hit the wall in a shower of sparks, which set the forest afire.

TABLET: CLX

When the flames licked the gas leaking from Optimus Prime's wreckage, he exploded. The forest collapsed around them, trapping El Krunko in the flames.

TABLET: CLXI

Once the forest had burned to ash, El Krunko arose to find that Shakespeare, and Quito von Libinschtein's rainbow squad were nowhere to be scene. Having nothing better to do, El Krunko made his way back to the Cave of Souls, and re-entered the foul place. Deep into the darkness of the cave he journeyed. Darkness followed... Darkness... Darkness... More darkness. Darkness. A bit of light. More darkness... Until... Two red dots appeared on the cave wall ahead. Then came the roar. A tremendous roar. One so great that it shook the planet itself.

"Odds Bodkins!" shrieked El Krunko, for there was Bruce: The Australian.

"G'day then El Krunko-mate. I been waitin' for ya a good many suns. I don't like waitin'. Guess I'll have to destroy ya then mate. No worries."

El Krunko grabbed at his chainsaw holster only to realize that his Ancestral weapon was still missing!

TABLET: CLXII

Bruce laughed at El Krunko's plight. He whipped out his Crocodile Dundee ™ brand knife, and rushed forward. Suddenly, in mid-dash, Bruce's chest exploded outward in a shower of blood and gore.

Amazed, El Krunko turned round to find his good friend Langust, smoking shotgun in hand. "Langust!" he chortled. "Where the hell have you been? Is my wife okay?"

"We were driven mad by our pasts," Langust replied. "Luckily I managed to find a confession booth, where the priest restored my wits. But we still have to find Pennsylvania and Elvis!"

"You're right!" El Krunko declared. "And my A.C. and Brunhilda! Onward!"

TABLET: CLXIII

Spurred by his found friend, El Krunko and Langust marched even deeper into the cave. For hours they trod, step by step, until they began to lose hope. At their darkest hour, only seconds before El Krunko would have truly given up his quest, the earth shook.

To their surprise, the ceiling of the cave grew red hot, and burst open. Hovering above them was Bumblebee, the meekest of the Transformers.

"Have you guys seen a red Mac-Truck?" he asked.

"You mean Optimus Prime? He's back that way." El Krunko pointed. With that, Bumblebee was off, and the two heroes climbed out from the cave, eager to spend some time in the upperworld. As they emerged into the light, a strange smell hit them.

"Mmmm..." drooled Langust. "Who's that?"

When they finally got to their feet, they were amazed to find a herd of burning pigs.

TABLET: CLXIV

El Krunko ripped off his shirt and cracked his knuckles. With the light of the sun beating down upon his bare chest, he uttered the words, "Heba-Meba-Jeba-Cow!" His Ancestral Chainsaw heeded the words of calling, but it had so distant, so far removed from its master's hands, that it accelerated to a velocity beyond its maximum limits. The A.C. flew right past El Krunko and collided with a wall 4 miles away. The Ancestral Chainsaw detonated in a nuclear explosion, and was transformed to dust, and radioactive rubble.

Now there *had* been legend of another Ancestral Chainsaw. The A.C. Mark II, and El Krunko, eager for a weapon worthy of his icy grip, began the quest to find the sacred weapon.

TABLET: CLXV

El Krunko and Langust traveled back to the Cave of Soul's entrance, and were shocked to find that it had collapsed. When El Krunko unlocked El Trucko and hopped in, they were further surprised to find Pennsylvania passed out in the front seat! After reviving her, she told them about how she was forced to eat Elvis Frankenstein while stark raving mad, and of how she thought he was a real chicken, and not a chicken mind in a tarred and feathered human body. Her wits were restored to her fully by means of a bottle of Pepto-Bismol, which she had found and drank after the grisly meal.

Relieved that his wife had been found, El Krunko had hot monkey sex with her, and together, the trio left the planet in El Trucko, in search of his new weapon.

TABLET: CLXVI

El Krunko set a course for the temple where he had originally received the first Ancestral Chainsaw. The temple was on the evil Planet of the Apes, which El Krunko despised. After a few days of star travel, the planet was spotted, and El Krunko set El Trucko down. Alas, once faced with the sealed entrance to the temple, El Krunko realized that it had been so long, he'd forgotten the secret password.

TABLET: CLXVII

El Krunko started to cry. Upon seeing the poor sobbing stranger, a kindly ape lumbered up to El Krunko, and asked the pathetic creature, "What is wrong, my friend?"

El Krunko blurted out, "I can't remember the password to the holy temple of Ancestry and Chainsaws."

The ape told him three things. Firstly, that the temple, under the new order of the Federal Bureau of Ancestry and Chainsaws, no longer needed a password. Secondly, that he needed a nice goatee if the Bureau was to take him seriously, and lastly, that he was a giant, walking, mother-fuck of a cock-suckin' asswipe, which to the apes was quite the compliment.

TABLET: CLXVIII

El Krunko, unaware that he was treated with proper courtesy, strangled the ape with his bare hands.

And so, El Krunko and our heroes entered the F.B.A.C. and filled out the required paperwork in triplicate. Upon submission, and a hefty processing fee, the apes relinquished possession of the Ancestral Chainsaw Mark II.

El Krunko graciously thanked them, and was about to leave, when suddenly an orangutan burst in. "He murdered Dr. Zaius!" the primate shouted, and he pointed to El Krunko.

TABLET: CLXIX

Without a moment to lose, El Krunko pulled the cord to rev up his A.C. Mark II, but the motor didn't turn over. As the apes bore down on him, El Krunko grinned nonchalantly, and pulled the cord once more, but still it didn't start. The apes laughed as they surrounded him.

"He'll never find the gas in the second room to the left down that hallway!" the tallest of the apes declared.

"Evolution wins again!" El Krunko retorted to the foolish Ape, before executing a flawless triple flip and landing in a somersault. Langust just jumped over them, and the two headed to the gas room to fill up his Ancestral Chainsaw Mark II's gas tank.

TABLET: CLXX

El Krunko and Langust locked themselves into the room and searched for the fuel, only to find that there were hundreds upon hundreds of canisters, all filled with different varieties of juices and potions. Pounding rang forth from the door, and it was clear by the sound of it that the irate primates wished to tear El Krunko's limbs off, and beat his stump with them.

El Krunko hunted through the tiny names scribbled on the top-left portion of the cans.

O.J. - Milk - Purple Stuff - "Ah ha!" Chainsaw Juice. El Krunko filled his A.C. Mark II with the precious liquid, and took an extra swig for himself. It only took one great pull of the cord for the engine to start right up, and the A.C. Mark II roared louder than the original ever did. El Krunko cackled in a large hearty and obnoxious voice that filled the room and scared Langust, who backed away into the corner. El Krunko's series of wild slashes occurred so fast, that Langust's eyes couldn't follow, but the end result was that El Krunko burst through the door, and slashed all of the apes in the general vicinity. All that remained was ape kibble (for the A.C. Mark II has a dehydration option on it).

This was Langust's chance, and like a true pig he was, he got down on all fours, and ate the monkey kibble as if it were a big prize. Everything seemed right with the world, until El Krunko felt something creeping down his leg.

My Godzilla! El Krunko thought to himself. *The Chainsaw Juice that I doth swig'th hath given me Anemic Dysentery* (chronic diarrhea for you non-science types). *I must find a way!* [to stop this].

TABLET: CLXXI

"Quick!" Langust tossed El Krunko an anti-laxative. "Drink this!" And just in time too, for more apes appeared, with Pennsylvania in tow.

"We have captured your woman," they said.

"Now submit to our trial."

"Very well," El Krunko said as he lowered his weapon. "I capitulate to your demands."

The apes were about to handcuff him, when a butch female voice broke the silence. "No. He's mine." And every last one of the apes burst into bloody chunks.

"Great Godzilla's Ghost!" El Krunko swore. "It can't be you! Not you! You died in the battle of Ofgur IV!"

But sure enough, standing before him was his old arch-enemy from childhood, the villainous La Krunka, armed with her Ancestral Buzzsaw.

TABLET: CLXXII

In the blink of an eye, La Krunka grabbed El Krunko and they both vanished, leaving Langust with the bits of bloody ape chunks (which did not turn to kibble). Meanwhile, El Krunko appeared in a room he had never seen before and La Krunka was nowhere in sight. El Krunko moved for the door, but found his feet were braced tight by metal clamps.

A growl which came from the shadows, and claws scraped the metal walls. "Chewie?" El Krunko hoped, but no. A big ugly bug-like creature came into the light. El Krunko scream in fright, and the bug-like thing moved in to consume him.

TABLET: CLXXIII

Just as the monster's fangs were inches away from El Krunko's head, it stopped. The monsters Id and Super-ego appeared on its shoulders. "Kill! Destroy!

Mangle!" said Id, "then go have sex with your sister!"

Before the monster could listen to its Id, the theme to ABC After School Special began to play, and his Super-ego spoke up. "Honor El Krunko," it said, and so the monster let him go.

TABLET: CLXXIV

Seeing the opportunity to smash and destroy, El Krunko ignored any imaginary people on his shoulder, and killed the bug thing, which was busy having an existential crisis. Having done this, El Krunko decided his prison cell was gettin' real tired, <u>real</u> fast.

El Krunko sat down to meditate, and was instantly transported to DeChronox V on the other side of the Universe: home to the fabled Quest o' Matic '76.

El Krunko needed a new purpose. A proper Quest more grand than any he'd undertaken before!

El Krunko approached the machine, a computer towering 10 stories tall with lights and readouts too numerous to count. At the main terminal, El Krunko filled in his name, company, and software protection I.D. number so that he could register online, and after the computer did its terrible dance, it spewed forth a quest upon a piece of paper similar to a fortune cookie fortune.

The fortune read: "Take o'er the Universe"
And he was off.

TABLET: CLXXV

"Taking over the Universe is no small task," El Krunko declared. "I need help." Catching the next Galactic Taxi –

- - - - - - - - - -
LOST TO THE AGES
- - - - - - - - - -

After burying his parents, El Krunko and his allies sought out Trunk Hall, the seal of the Trunkian government. El Krunko burst in and proclaimed, "By rightful law, as I've previously established, this planet is mine!!"

El Qurunko, the President of Trunk, gladly gave El Krunko the deed to the planet (He had wanted to retire for many years).

El Qurunko cried out, "I'm going to Phisbee Land!"

With his home planet now firmly and legally under his control, El Krunko traveled to the Trunkian Military Command HQ to make preparations for future conquests on his quest to take over the Universe. He quickly found General El Punko, and with Sparky in tow, ordered a draft to be held. El Punko was skeptical at first, but after Sparky chewed his leg a bit, he gave in.

TABLET: CLXXVI

The people flocked to the cause, for they would be the leaders of the New Order. The planet was soon in a blood thirsty rampage. El Krunko went to Planet Trunk's main control center, hopped in the drivers seat, and aimed towards the nearest inhabited planet, Fizzy.

Fizzy was a calm planet with a kind, friendly, open, and highly intelligent populace, all part of an autonomous collective where everyone participated equally in the betterment of their entire race. They were also cute and fuzzy.

Needless to say, when the two planets collided, and the Krunkii of Trunk poured over, the cute inhabitants were quickly slaughtered in a bordello of blood.

With this first warm-up victory achieved, both planets started driving to the next planet, where from there it would be on to the next.

The Revolution, as it would later come to be called, had begun.

TABLET: CLXXVII

In the days, weeks, and months that followed, civilized planet after civilized planet fell to the supreme military strategies of El Krunko.

Millions of years of enlightenment, culture, and knowledge were lost forever.

Thousands of wise texts were destroyed.

The most brilliant minds of the galaxy were killed.

El Krunko laughed hysterically.

TABLET: CLXXVIII

While in his hysteria, El Krunko happened to glance at his feet, where the fortune that sent him on his quest had fallen. "Take o'er the Universe" it read.

Suddenly it hit him.

"O'er," was a trademark of Shakespeare, whose razor sharp wit had nearly killed him once before. And El Krunko knew, just as everyone knows, that Shakespeare writes sentence with ten syllables, and not six.

El Krunko picked up the fortune, and realized the second half was folded back. He opened the paper, and it now read, "Take o'er the Universe in your own dreams."

While he had been enjoying taking over the Universe, he decided to put his current ambitions on hiatus in lieu of following the wishes of the Quest o' Matic '76.

El Krunko grabbed his bunny rabbit, and went to sleep.

What season was it? T'was Summer. T'was night.

El Krunko awoke, but he was asleep,
And that's when he knew, he could retreat.
The dream was a ploy of Shakespeare's essay,
To spin a sequel to his evil play.
El Krunko was screwed. Nothing else to say.
He became an actor in Shakespeare's play.

"A Mid Summer Nights Dream II - The Endless Ocean of Blood and Gore."

TABLET: CLXXIX

El Krunko tried desperately not to fall deeper into his slumber, but he could not suppress his exhaustion. In his magical delirium, El Krunko became aware of his spirit floating in an infinite purple void.

"Welcome to my play, El Krunko! Ha! Ha!" The voice of Shakespeare echoed throughout the space, and the purple void began to collect and coalesce, until it morphed into the gigantic head of Shakespeare.

"And welcome to your doom! Mwa ha ha ha!" Shakespeare cried, and thousands upon thousands of tiny razor sharp wits flew at El Krunko at incredible speeds. El Krunko raised up his arms in terror.

TABLET: CLXXX

One after another, the wits slashed and pierced El Krunko. He screamed in agony until they all vanished. "Muah ha ha ha ha! Ha ha ha ha ha!" the head laughed.

"You're nothing more than a coward," El Krunko indignantly replied. "Look you big projected head, send me back to Kansas or I'll pull you out from your booth, and flay you alive."

The head of Shakespeare vanished and the purple haze returned.

"That's more like it!" said our her, when he heard a strange melody in the distance. The song was coming closer and closer, and growing louder and louder. El Krunko faintly made out a car. As it approached, El Krunko realized that Jimi Hendrix was heading straight for him at 80 mph.

TABLET: CLXXXI

Wham! El Krunko was struck by the Forger Of Rock. "That ain't cool," spoke Hendrix. "Let me get you outta this purple haze, man. I know it like the back of my hand."

Unfortunately, Hendrix was stoned, so the two of them wandered aimlessly in the dream for a couple hours. El Krunko, the mental giant that he was, decided to wake up. Hendrix music was blasting when he woke, and his right arm was missing. Where was it?

He recited the magic words, "Heba-Meba-Jeba-Cow," to no result. He had to find his arm.

TABLET: CLXXXII

Determined to find the missing limb, El Krunko wandered the barren landscape for what seemed like minutes. After a short while, El Krunko collapsed, exhausted and depressed.

Where am I? This isn't Trunk's main control center! he thought to himself. *Am I still asleep? I'll never find my appendage again!* Just then he noticed a trail of toilet paper leading away from his feet. He traced it back to a public bathroom, and leapt headfirst into the toilet.

He surfed the sewer and eventually reached its end... the evil fortress of the Rat King! He knew this was a forsaken place, as many mouse heads, shrunken yet noticeable, lined the fence to the fortress. "I've indeed entered on unholy ground! May my Krunkian bloodline give me luck!"

TABLET: CLXXXIII

His luck was indeed with him, for there laying on the floor of the underground lair, was his right arm. After sewing it back on, El Krunko flexed to make sure it worked properly. But when he looked up, a strange fog had fallen upon the room.

"What ho!" he cried. "What devilry is this?" A hearty laugh echoed all around him. "Shakespeare!" he cried. "Damn thee!"

TABLET: CLXXXIV

Shakespeare stepped out of the mist, revved up his iambic pentameter, and declared, "The PURPLE was but an inkling of what / I truly am! Behold my final form!"

Shakespeare ripped away his human skin, and revealed that he was truly, a Purple (gasp!) Aardvark! But Shakespeare was not as El Krunko remembered the Purple Aardvarks to be. He was instead a new, hideous breed, with deformed yet highly developed muscles and facial features. An army of similar beings appeared behind Shakespeare, while more parachuted in from manholes up above.

And though El Krunko had sworn to destroy all Purple Aardvarks by himself, he could not face this horde alone.

This was truly a Krunkian quandary.

TABLET: CLXXXV

"Alas!" cried El Krunko.

"Oh, so you're Scottish, eh?" the Purple Aardvark lord Shakespeare barked. "Then it's the Scottish play for you! I'll get my Scottish henchmen to finish you off!" He clenched his fists, highly insulted, having thought El Krunko called him a little girl.

As Shakespeare's henchmen raced forward, swords in hand, and El Krunko found himself in his darkest hour, with no hope for victory, Rowdy Roddy Piper and Brett the Hit Man Hart entered to bagpipe music, having come straight from Monday Nitro WCW Wrestling Slamboree.

TABLET: CLXXXVI

* * * * * * * * * *

"The End." Sing Potato finished.

Happy sat up in his armchair sofa in the Planet Ethnocentric Dracula II main palace throne room of Captain King El Krunko II, for during the Epic, Happy convinced El Krunko II that he should combine a few of his leftover styles, and allowed himself to be dubbed, "Captain King El Krunko the Second," since he was just a time-stream tangent from the original El Krunko, in Happy's own original Universe.

"Wow, so that's your past." Happy nodded politely. "What do you think of it all?" Happy inquired upon his Captain King, who was leaning against his time-copy Ancestral Chainsaw, while sitting on a throne made out of empty beer cans.

El Krunko II looked up in a drunken stupor. "Huh? Oh whatever, I read it before."

Happy leapt to his feet and screamed in fury. "Then what the fuck was the point of us wasting all this time listening to it? I never even cared about what happened to *you* ages ago! This is *my* Epic, and I want to go back to the past to save the REAL El Krunko! ... Although that does explain about the mysterious Purple Aardvark civilization, and fills in a lot of other important plot holes and backstory. But wait a second! Last time I remembered, back in my time-stream, the Purple Aardvarks were still alive... I guess that means aside from Shakespeare's Purple Aardvark Mutations, Bob the Martyr being killed really WAS the downfall of the Purple Aardvark civilization. That's fucking ironic as hell. Brilliant work El Krunko!"

El Krunko II spit out his chaw. "I have no idea what you're talking about. But thanks."

Planet E.D. rumbled a bit, and proclaimed in a planetary fashion, "Is it over yet?"

Happy raised his fist in the air, and jumped up and down on the official Planet E.D. control platform. "Yes, it's over! Did you know he'd already heard it? Why did we bother listening to it? Don't you all realize that we're just gonna have to do it all over again when the original El Krunko has to hear it?"

"Big deal!" El Krunko II said as he cracked open another beer and downed it in one heaving gulp. "It's a bitchin' story, and I liked it."

"Oh, sure! Easy for you to say!" Happy shouted. "The Epic's not spoken by *your* eyeball!"

"Besides. Your El Krunko won't ever hear it anyway. He's dead remember." El Krunko II burped. "We can't save him. I told you. It's... It's against time-law! Right E.D.?"

The planet responded, "Whatever."

"That's it! I've had enough of this!" Happy was in a frenzy." I don't care what you said about not being able to save El Krunko! We have to try to save him!"

El Krunko II tried to protest, but had had one too many. Instead he spewed vomit, and fell over unconscious.

"It's settled then!" Happy said. "Planet E.D. Set time matrix coordinates for when we last left, 15 minutes before."

"But I thought we couldn't do that!" Planet E.D. nervously quacked.

"Fuck it!" Happy punched the big red button, and with that, the control platform flew into the sky, and in a flurry of lights, and beeps, exploded into the realm of time travel.

* * * * * * * * * *

"Well," Happy explained. "You know how you've always felt Ethnocentric? I finally understand why you felt so complete in your existence. For I am now both Happy... and happy!" He beamed with joy.

"But," E.D. replied, "Your name isn't actually Happy. It's Barry."

TABLET: CLXXXVII

Miguel Sanchez dropped his mocha latte on the floor in shock, and nearly choked on the last bite of his penultimate leftover strawberry jammie. "You're Barry Happypants!!?" he shouted at the top of his lungs, as everyone shut up and looked warily at him.

"Umm... well I prefer Happy. 'Specially now that I'm so happy these days, and all, and it's ever so fitting. But yes, that is who I once was, what I think might have been many aeons ago, but I can't be so sure, because–"

Miguel Sanchez interrupted him. "Quiet fool. I have a message for you."

El Krunko whispered in E.D.'s ear, "I thought that pig's name sounded familiar. But I thought Barry Happypants was killed by Gribulor? I saw him one time at the museum."

Ethnocentric Dracula quietly spoke in El Krunko's ear. "He was. Shhh."

Miguel stepped back, and started fishing through his pocket, while Happy mindlessly noshed on the bag of Baco-Cruncho's he picked up from a vending machine a few minutes earlier. He'd toss them in the air, and follow their nifty rainbow trails into his mouth. "Rainbow power kicks ass," he declared.

Miguel spoke as searched his pockets... "One of my many clones questfully took on an Epic quest, and when he failed, I swore vengeance to avenge his death, and complete what he had begun, but had not done. I thought the chance would never arise, but now it finally has! And I, TK-421, will surely succeed where so many Sanchii have failed in the past, because of failure!" The other three heroes had no idea what he was talking about, and impatiently waited for him to get to the point. Miguel Sanchez smiled as his hand finally gripped what he had been hastily searching for in his coat pockets. "The death of Barry Happypants! FOR GRIBULOR!"

When suddenly, the world was plummeted into darkness. All four of them stopped, and looked up, for high above them a huge planet had appeared in orbit.

TABLET: CLXXXVIII

Huge missiles fired from the huge planet, and down from orbit came El Krunko II aboard his snazzy surfboard. The missiles impacted the planet's surface, causing explosions all around the heroes. "Noooooooo!" Miguel cried out. "My warrior clones!" For indeed, the missiles had been fired exactly where the clones had come out previously, that is, where they had come out earlier, in the other time-stream, or rather in this time-stream, or another version of it, where... Regardless, the clones were all exploded, along with the war machines that carried them.

El Krunko II surfed down and beheaded Miguel

Sanchez Clone TK-421 with one swipe of his alternative Ancestral Chainsaw. El Krunko stared in amazement at his elder self, and El Krunko II slapped him five and spoke, "I am indeed you, El Krunko, from one possible future. There's no time to explain. We must find the Red Monkey Shaman. And this time, Happy, don't kill him!"

Happy stood there dumbstruck, and was whisked away by El Krunko aboard his snazzy surfboard, which was the same snazzy surfboard as El Krunko II, of course, but not as old, and therefore with less rust, and wear and tear, and such.

Now one might well ask, having reached this strange juncture in our story, how both El Krunkos, much less their surfboards, could possibly exist simultaneously in one time-stream. Would not both El Krunkos finally realize the horror of the Lacanian split between self and other, literalized in the body before them, that is both them, and not-them, and go mad, reduced to some blabbering infant-like condition? Would not they both explode in a shower of anti-matter, since they were both of the same matter, yet existing in simultaneous time and space? Or would not, perhaps, the very fabric of space and time be ripped apart by this paradoxical situation?

The great mathematician-philosopher Scienrontus, in his treatise, "The Epic of Space and Time," truly the culmination of his life's work, remarks on situations such as these. Unfortunately, that Epic, like so many before it, has been lost to the ages, and we shall just have to trust what little we know of Scienrontus and temporal physics. Now, back to our story.

TABLET: CLXXXIX

Flying through the air at tremendous speeds, it was mere moments until both El Krunkos, Happy, and Ethnocentric Dracula arrived at the group of Red Monkey Shamans doing their dance around a fire.

When Happy stepped forward, the monkeys suddenly stopped, and turned towards him. One came forward and pointed a thin, bent finger at the hero.

"Barry Happypants," it croaked, "do you not remember me, the Red Monkey Shaman Higgle-de?"

Impossible, Happy thought. *This cannot be Higgle-de, for when I met him last, he was young and full of vigor.*

"I hear the words in your mind," the Shaman said. "I have grown strong with age, and my magical talents have increased tenfold since last we met. The secret of how to traverse time and space instantaneously is in my hand, but I was foolish... and I did not realize that even when one travels to another time... one still ages normally... But no matter."

Captain King El Krunko II bellowed out a hearty laugh and whipped out his alternative Ancestral Chainsaw. El Krunko followed suit, and Happy stood dumbfounded.

"I, Captain King El Krunko, hereby claim this planet, to be destroyed at my disposal!" And with a mighty swing, El Krunko II lopped Higgle-de's head clean off.

Happy stood and stared. "I thought we didn't want him killed?" Captain King El Krunko II laughed louder and louder, enjoying the use of his proper style.

El Krunko cried out, "I do believe that's maniacal laughter!"

The Captain King continued to laugh as he slew the remaining Red Monkeys. "Foolish mortals!" he cried. "Now, with the destruction of Higgle-de, there is no one left to stop Gribulor, except for me and my time-double! The Universe will tremble before the might of El Krunko times two!" and with that, the entire planet began to shake with force.

El Krunko backed away. "He's mad. We must slay him, but how can we possibly defeat El Krunko? It's damn near impossible, if I do say so myself."

Happy shook with fear. "Then what are we to do? El Krunko has no weakness!

"El Krunko has *one* weakness!" a voice spoke from the heavens (It was Planet Ethnocentric Dracula, who had grown tired of El Krunko II's antics). "I've read his Epic! His undoing is to be his left foot pinky toe!" Meanwhile the planet continued to shake in its death throes.

"Bwa hahahahaha!" Captain King El Krunko II laughed. "I had that toe chopped off as a precaution, the first time I read my Epic!"

With their chances for victory removed, Happy and El Krunko started to cry... when suddenly a time portal opened up!

Out stepped El Krunko III, who sported a goatee, and Ethnocentric Dracula III, who donned 3 mauls in each of his 3 hands, and they made short work of the maniacally evil villain, and Captain King El Krunko II was no more.

El Krunko III exclaimed triumphantly, "We must get out of here! There's no time to lose!"

And with that they were off!

They scooped up Langust, Grunta-Grunta-Pow-Wow, and HK-48, all of whom had appeared in the insta-safe, and they soon arrived on Planet Ethnocentric Dracula to greet the real Happy Barrypants (and not the one from the past, who had arrived with El Krunko, Ethnocentric Dracula, their sidekicks, El Krunko III, and Ethnocentric Dracula III [who could not be mistaken.]).

Just then, as they said their hellos, the planet below exploded.

The Happy from the past (although it's currently the present), whom we shall refer to as Happy Ib cried forth, "It's my twin!"

The real Happy, the one who'd traveled across dimensions and returned, whom we shall refer to as Happy Ia smiled. "Totally brotha. So, how'd you like learning about your past, and raising your power level from touching the Orb of the Drunken Wanderer?"

Past Happy Ib scratched his head and shrugged, "I guess I missed the chance."

The group sighed as they viewed the newly formed Asteroid Belt.

"Then there's no other option!" El Krunko III screamed.

And with that he was off to the official Planet E.D. control platform. "Set time matrix coordinates for right after the Sanchinator exploded."

The control platform flew into the sky, and in a flurry of lights, and beeps, exploded into the realm of time travel.

* * * * * * * * * *

Miguel Sanchez smiled as his hand finally gripped what he had been hastily searching for in his coat pockets. "The death of Barry Happypants! FOR

GRIBULOR!"

When suddenly, the world was plummeted into darkness. All four of them stopped, and looked up, for high above them a huge planet had appeared in orbit.

TABLET: CXC

Huge missiles fired from the planet, and down from orbit came El Krunko II aboard his snazzy surfboard. The missiles impacted the planet's surface, causing explosions all around the heroes. "Noooooooo!" Miguel cried out. "My warrior clones!"

Suddenly the group grew silent, for high above them, a second Planet Ethnocentric Dracula gloriously appeared in orbit!

TABLET: CXCI

Happy Ia cried out in hysterics, "This is madness! Now there will be three of me! This is all your doing El Krunkos!"

El Krunko and El Krunko III turned towards Happy Ia, whose eyes were glazed over with madness and fury. Happy Ia seized the controls of the Planet.

"What are you doing? No, you fool!" shrieked El Krunko shockingly, and he grabbed for Happy Ia's arms. The two struggled over the controls, and the planet lurched about, and smashed into the other Planet Ethnocentric Dracula.

The two planets shattered into countless pieces, and all aboard them were vaporized.

Far below, on the planet's surface, Happy Ic, El Krunko Ib, Ethnocentric Dracula Ib, and Miguel Sanchez Clone TK-421 Ib watched the conflagration in amazement.

Happy Ic came to his senses, and slew Miguel Sanchez Clone TK-421 Ib.

"Take that villain!" he cried out.

"Urk!" Miguel Sanchez Clone TK-421 Ib croaked, and then he croaked.

"Much strangeness has happened here today, more than perhaps even we know." El Krunko Ib declared. "Let us abandon any hope for understanding the mystery of today, and consider ourselves the lone and solitary survivors of a terrible battle that spanned the heavens. Plus, we should get the hell outta here."

And away they flew, without their styles, aboard El Krunko's snazzy surfboard, until their attention was drawn by a group of Red Monkeys dancing and singing around a fire.

They landed, and one of the Red Monkey Shamans came forward.

"Barry Happypants," it croaked, "do you not remember me, the Red Monkey Shaman Higgle-de?"

Impossible, Happy thought. *This cannot be Higgle-de, for when I met him last, he was young and full of vigor.*

"I hear the words in your mind," the Shaman said. "I have grown strong with age, and my magical talents have increased tenfold since last we met. The secret of how to traverse time and space instantaneously is in my hand, but I was foolish... and I did not realize that even when one travels to another time... one still ages normally... But no matter."

A sign! Happy thought. *Perhaps this is the way I will defeat Gribulor!*

"I know nothing of that," the Red Monkey Shaman said.

"Then what use are you?" Happy asked.

"I will tell you this," the R.M.S. replied. "Go now, and quickly, to the Pleasure Planet Epsilon Omicron Five, and there must you visit the most beautiful girl in the Universe. You will not regret this."

"Sounds good to me," El Krunko said, and off the trio went.

TABLET: CXCII

As they were about to break into orbit, Happy pointed down at a strange glow which was looming on the horizon. Down, down, down they surfed until they reached the source of the light.

Happy hopped off the surfboard, and he felt a strange presence was close. But when he finally stood upon the very spot from which the strange energy was emanating, nothing was to be found.

Then... slowly... A shimmering form appeared before him.

It was an orb, strangely familiar to his sight, and it glew a primordial green.

"The orb of the Drunken Wanderer!" Happy whispered. He cautiously reached out and grasped it. His hands clung to the orb as if attracted by some magnetic force. A power coursed through him causing his hair to stand on end. Images flashed in his mind. Images of the ancient past, of the tale of Lothar Happypants and Briguvor, images of his own past, as a mercenary assassin, trained by the Og Corp. and oft hired by the unscrupulous leaders of the Red Monkey civilization. Then came visions of the future, when Gribulor the Great Goat-Man would face him in final, earth-shattering combat.

When the shock of power stopped, Happy blacked out.

El Krunko and Ethnocentric Dracula stood about confused.

When they were about to just toss Happy and the orb on the surfboard, and make their way to see the hot chicks, a diamond time portal opened up, and appearing before them was El Krunko IV and Ethnocentric Dracula IV, who bore no facial hair, but *were* dressed in flashy time-police outfits.

EL Krunko IV and E.D. IV raised their Ancestral Pistols at El Krunko and Ethnocentric Dracula. "Hands up!" they cried. El Krunko and E.D. willingly obliged.

El Krunko IV walked over to Happy, and prodded him lightly with the end of his boot. "This is him alright," El Krunko IV said. "The primary cause of all those temporal disturbances."

E.D. IV pulled out a pair of handcuffs and spoke loudly and clearly, "You're both under arrest for time-crimes. You have the right to shut up, and the right to a fair trial of your time-peers under the jurisdiction of the Intertimensional Criminal Courts."

"We're in for it now," E.D. quacked sadly. El Krunko merely moaned as he was put on his stomach and shackled.

El Krunko IV radioed in to headquarters. "This is time-team Krunko calling in. We've got them. Have the other suspects been detained?"

"Yes. Return to base immediately."

"Very well," El Krunko IV replied into his handset. "Bag 'em and tag 'em'!" And Ethnocentric Dracula IV, his partner, knocked their prisoners, our heroes, unconscious.

When they finally woke up, they discovered they were in a large holding cell.

The occupants of this legendary cell were/are (since it's outside of time): the Red Monkey Shaman Higgle-de, El Krunko, Happy Ia, Ib, and Ic, Ethnocentric Dracula, El Krunko II and El Krunko III, Ethnocentric Dracula III, two sets of Langusts, Grunta-Grunta-Pow-Wow's, and HK-48's, and two computer screens that showed both Planet Ethnocentric Dracula's in a strange starless orbit, both covered in black and white striped tarps.

TABLET: CXCIII

And so they waited for what seemed like both an eternity, and a single second, for time had no meaning in the Intertimensional Criminal Courts. They were brought before a time-judge, who heard each of their stories in turn. The time-judge's mind was taxed by the tale, even though he'd judged so many Intertimensional problems before. The time-jury's debate was short.

Guilty, across the board.

But Happy Ic, El Krunko Ib, and E.D. Ib had a plan. No sooner was the verdict spoken, that the three of them leapt into the crowd, and ripped everyone except the prisoners to shreds.

"We should have thought of that!" El Krunko III said, for he the others remained forever in their bonds.

Happy Ic, El Krunko Ib, and E.D. Ib abandoned their styles as quickly as their former companions / time-alternates, and head for the exit.

"Escape!" Happy cried out, and the group ran down the hall and into an Intertimensional Taxi.

"Forward!" El Krunko declared, and forward they went.

"Stop!" he declared again, when some time had passed. The taxi stopped, and out they went.

All around them was a great ocean, and they stood on a small island, with one palm tree in the middle.

"Damnation!" El Krunko said.

"The surfboard!" Happy cried out.

"Its gone!" El Krunko replied.

"We seem!'" Happy said.

"To Only!" El Krunko replied.

"Speak!" Happy replied.

"In Short!" El Krunko said.

"Sentences!" Happy finished. For now they saw that the punishment of the court had been decided, and despite their escape, they were still afflicted with the consequences of its decision.

TABLET: CXCIV

The Triumphant Trio stood around pondering their predicament, when they heard a sound... "What," Happy spoke.

"Is," E.D. quacked.

"That?" El Krunko queried... as the taxi flew off.

"Shit!" El Krunko declared.

"We're," E.D. pointed at the taxi.

"stranded................. forever!" Happy cried, then he fell to his knees, and sobbed.

"Hey!" Sing Potato announced from his holographic image.

In order: El Krunko, E.D, then Happy.

"It's!"

"Sing!"

"Potato!"

"Yes," Sing Potato said... and very slowly pronounced, "We are still outside time. Now's the chance to tell El Krunko the Epic!"

In the same order they cried aloud,

"You're!"

"Fucking!"

"Mad!"However El Krunko wanted to hear it anyway, and so, at a pace 50 times slower than last time, as Sing Potato was also afflicted by the jury's decision, the Epic of El Krunko was again recited.

An eternity, and a 5 o'clock shadow later...

TABLET: CXCV

The trio was still stranded. After a ponderous time spent lamenting over their fate, (for each could only speak a few syllables at a time,) El Krunko cried out, "Fuck... ... ... this." He lifted up Happy and E.D. above his head, and surfed upon his feet across the vast sea of time, until finally land could be seen.

Over the course of the long voyage, Happy had asked El Krunko whether his Epic had any effect on him. El Krunko replied that yes, he now had to discover how his parents had died. This conversation took nearly their entire trip, although to be fair, the crashing waves blunted the force of their words, and much repetition was necessary.

When they finally reached land, a group of savages stood before them on the beach. One savage spoke, but his words were incomprehensible. Ethnocentric Dracula said, "They... are... much...

different... than... I! ... Death... to... them... all!" and attacked furiously.

Happy and El Krunko shrugged, and joined him in battle.

It was brief.

TABLET: CXCVI

But Ethnocentric Dracula's conversation after the battle was not. It gave the savages time to regroup their vast armies upon the eastern most front of the Savage Frontier, as it was later to be called. For many weeks the trio battled an unending onslaught of dirty un-evolved mammals, akin to dwarves, but as tall as men. Amidst the long lasting carnage, El Krunko had time to reflect upon his true history. El Krunko wept with happiness as he realized that he had three loves: Carnage was one, and the other two were Pennsylvania, and Brunhilda, both of whom he now pledged to locate and nail.

At one point, El Krunko stood upon a barricade mounted of dead savages, and writ in some stone that he picked up, that he now had 2 extra loves... Epics, and Time Travel.

Ethnocentric Dracula finished off the final savage, and tallied his count. "That's... two... hundred... thousand... five... sixty... seven."

Happy Barrypants laughed furiously, and announced his victory, at a clean "Million and five."

El Krunko conceded victory to Happy, and with that they were off into the heart of the strange land.

TABLET: CXCVII

And what a strange land it was, stranger, in fact, than any other seen in the experiences of the trio. In this land the flowers were ashen gray, and they smelled of freshly manufactured automobiles. The trees were bright purple, and gave off a sap that tasted of whiskey.

"This,"

"land,"

"is,"

"wondrous,"

"strange." they took turns in saying.

El Krunko, upon tasting the sap of one of the trees, snapped it in half. The tree's liquid sprayed forth, and he sated his thirst, getting drunk in the process. He staggered along drunkenly, climbing a steep mountain as his companions gave chase. But when El Krunko reached the summit, he found himself teetering on the edge of a volcano, with a field of blue lava bubbling beneath him.

"NOOOO!" he cried as he fell over the edge. Sploosh! was the sound he made as he hit the bubbling fluid. E.D. and Happy stared down in horror, when suddenly, El Krunko appeared from the depths.

"Its cold!" he cried up to them. "And... ... ... refreshing!"

E.D. and Happy leapt into the cool lava, and the three played Marco Polo to their hearts content.

TABLET: CXCVIII

After it was decided that Ethnocentric Dracula was the definitive winner of the game (though he secretly cheated many times by using his Godly power to transform into lava, that he might not be touched), they emerged somewhat heartbroken that their play time was over.

El Krunko erected a sign, and writ upon it, "Fun N' Games Volcano," while Happy and E.D. looked out upon the Savage Frontier.

"What... now?" El Krunko queried as he finished drawing a picture of the trio playing in the blue depths. Just then, in the far distance, a bright flash lit the heavens!

"Duck!" E.D. screamed!

"N!" Happy replied hastily.

"Cover!" El Krunko demanded, and the three of them dropped to the ground, and hid their eyes in the crooks of their shoulders from the ensuing explosion. Whiskey trees, purple flowers, savage corpses, and berry bushes galore crashed against their backs, but not once did they look up.

When the sounds of the bewildering destruction finally settled to a mere whimper, they stood upon their feet, and reassessed their surroundings. The once magnificent and wondrous strange land had been instantly transformed to rubble and debris. Upon the horizon a mushroom cloud of Epic proportions was blooming in its cadaverous splendor.

Without a word their course of action was decided, and moments later the Triumphant Trio found themselves at the base of the enormous mushroom. Beneath its cover most horrible, many other mushrooms had begun to grow at abnormal speeds, although instead of being as black as moonless nights, and as dark as E.D.'s dark dark soul (which had blackened since their time in Hell [though he was still no longer a Nubian.]), the mushrooms were bright festive colors.

Hundreds of thousands of fast forming festive fungi in cacophonies of whites, and blues, and greens, and incredible rainbow hues, littered the vast shadowed floors of the Epic mushroom. Water from the upper atmosphere that had collected upon the most-high spores of the fungus tower, rained down over its sides in tiny rivers, and had created a swamp of diabolical perfection for these many magic mushies to grow unchecked.

Before El Krunko or E.D. could stop him, Happy, in an elated stupor only a pig could appreciate, let alone comprehend, leapt from their tactical position behind one of the larger Christmas-like sections of the mushrooms, and began to wildly gorge himself on the cadaverous blooms. Ethnocentric Dracula was violently disgusted, and could hardly watch the grotesque ritual taking place before him, but El Krunko, starving after their days of battle, and also having a serious case of the munchies since he was still drunk on sap, dove into the fray of endless eating as well.

"Great ethnocentric ethnocentrism!" E.D. cried. "They've gone mushroom mad!"

TABLET: CXCIX

After thoroughly gorging himself, Happy sat happily, and plumply, under the shade of one of the larger mushrooms. His stomach rumbled. "Ooohhh..." he said. "Me... no... feel... good."

El Krunko looked up, his mouth foaming with spittle and mushroom juice, and together, the two vomited violently, and continuously.

But when they finished, the mounds of vomit stood up in manlike forms!

"Great... Gribulor's... Ghost!" Happy cried out.

"The Legendary,"

"Dreaded,"

"Fungus-Vomit,"

"Demons of,"

"Garner-Vor!" the trio all said (for they were becoming quite proficient in completing each other's thoughts). E.D. attacked first, but his fists of fury merely passed through the demon's grotesque liquid forms. The demons laughed with a deep, sickening, gurgling, guttural, groan.

"Zounds!" El Krunko cried out, for it was apparent that the demons would not be defeated by normal means. The monstrosities of Garner-Vor sprayed horrible gloop from their arms at the heroes, who soon became stuck fast in the mess.

The demons cackled once more, and lifted the three above their heads.

"To Garner-Vor!" they agreed, and ran off with the captured heroes in tow.

TABLET: CC

As they traveled through the mushroom forest, which seemed to grow upwards and outwards in every direction, a strange thing happened. El Krunko grew to half of his former height, while Happy tripled in size and stature. The weight of Happy overtook the vomit demons that were carrying him, and it became necessary for them to manufacture a wheelbarrow of vomit to ease their journey.

Hours passed, and the terrain continued to warp and twist around them. Opalescent tri-colored flowers budded, bloomed, and withered away by the dozens.

Mysterious shadows played within the dancing darkness of the eerie garden. Whirling winds howled, and scary music filled the air. And worst yet, a horrible stench, far worse indeed than the odor of their foul blobular cohorts which covered the heroes bodies thoroughly, rose up in the air. Ethnocentric Dracula promptly vomited and fell unconscious, but Happy and El Krunko were, of course, unaffected.

I have strange plans in mind. Happy pondered. *There is madness afoot.*

Soon they were all at the entrance of the Garner-Vor Immigration and Customs checkpoint. As the leader of the crack Vomit Bounty Hunter Squad which had captured the trio stepped forward to place his tentacle on the identification device, El Krunko hatched a plan of his own. Though miniature, he twirled and break-danced in fiendish confusion, and ate all the remaining vomit.

Their freedom had been attained, however gross it may have been to achieve.

"Freedom!" Happy cried aloud, in a deep, deep tone, for his voice had changed with his size.

"Duh," El Krunko squeaked.

The doorway lurched open...

TABLET: CCI

Alas, their freedom was not yet truly secured. For there, across the checkpoint and before them, stood another crack unit, this time one of the Garner-Vor Homeland Security Vomit Squads.

"Get 'em!" blurbled the squad leader.

El Krunko and Happy battled to the best of their ability, but any blow that struck the vomit demons merely passed through them.

"Eat 'em!" Happy cried out.

"I can't..." El Krunko moaned. "I'm... too... full... In... fact... I almost... fear that... I will... burst... Agh!" Just then, El Krunko's stomach started to grow, and was forced outwards like a balloon being blown. He cried out in pain as it exploded, sending stomach juices everywhere. The juices sprayed the vomit demons, and they began to melt.

"Nooooo! I'm melting! Meellttting..." they all blurbled and bloaned.

"Ha ha! Freedom is ours once more!" Happy said over the course of a few minutes. But then, as he looked down at his ally El Krunko, he discovered his friend was dead.

TABLET: CCII

Yes, Ethnocentric Dracula had unfortunately passed away while in his unconscious stupor. Happy leaned down, pulled out a monocle from his pocket, and held it in front of E.D.'s mouth. After inspecting it for moisture and finding none, he placed the monocle in his own good eye, and slowly addressed El Krunko, who was gathering up the last of his guts.

"My good sir. We are now a Dynamic Duo."

El Krunko pulled his pants up, and fastened his belt three notches tighter. "Tis Pity... Let's Go." They both looked at the corpse of Ethnocentric Dracula, shrugged, and passed through the gates into the mysterious foreign land. As would be expected, many a foul adventure followed. Vomit was eaten, treasures were stolen, and magnificent works of art were accidentally set aflame.

Eventually the duo found themselves at the base of a wide chasm. Far beneath them was a large box that emitted an unusual humming sound. It took nearly four days, and the remainder of their dried vomit rations (for in the time they had spent in Garner-Vor, they found it was the only edible substance, and had become quite proficient in re-preparing it), until they reached the large box.

Writ in large brown letters on the side of the box, was, "Property of the Intertimensional Criminal Justice System." Elation! They had come across something belonging to the bastards that stole their counterparts, their planets, and their Ancestral Weaponry (not to mention their ability to speak in long sentences.) El Krunko climbed to the top of the crate, and undid its fancy bow. As the wooden planks fell to the side, and revealed the unholy cargo within, the true mischievous malevolence of the justice system finally reared its ugly head.

At long last, the Dynamic Duo finally knew what the hell was going on, and what they had to do.

TABLET: CCIII

"Great... Gribulor's... Ghost!" Happy muttered. "It... was... Gribulor... all... along!"

There before them was the proof. Inside the chest was a huge pile of Goat-Man money, more than anyone could possibly afford to bribe the Intertimensional Criminal Justice System... Anyone except Gribulor, the Great Goat-Man, that is!

"We must... find... Gribulor... and... end... this... madness!" El Krunko suggested.

After looking around, the duo found a suitable

2x4, and off they surfed. As they left the atmosphere of Garner-Vor, they reverted to original sizes.

"Kick-ass!" Happy exclaimed.

Off they sailed into the sunset... or rather, towards the blazing hot white sun around which could be found the aforementioned planet of the Great Goat-Men. As they traveled to the planet, the duo gritted their teeth, and made really mean faces, while preparing for Epic battle.

TABLET: CCIV

Deep, deep into space they surfed. Past the Great Torrential Meteor Storm, and the Horrible Ice Comet Cascades, through the Flaming Fire Nebula, beyond the Notoriously Deadly Marshmallow Moons, and deeper still into the darkest reaches of the Great Timeless Cosmic Void.

As they hurtled onward, the passage of their travel into the deepest nether regions of the Galaxy of Time transformed into a symbolic journey within Happy's mind. Each moon they careened past represented a lock within the halls of his memories. Each Great Meteor they barely dodged represented a doorway waiting to be opened within those very same halls. Each Fiery Nebula they pulled gnarly tricks through represented the keys to those very same locks. The Vast Marshmallow wasteland represented Happy's gnawing hunger. And finally, the Great Timeless Cosmic Void they were venturing into, was beginning to take shape.... into the psychological map that he required!

"Yes!!! Behold!!!" Happy began to vibrate uncontrollably. His muscles tensed and started to ripple, and space rocks that were caught up in their surf's gravitational field collided against each other, creating a spectacle of miniature explosions all around them.

El Krunko, being Lord of the Slay, was oblivious to the seemingly harmless, and fairly boring commotion, and was concentrating solely upon his surfing ability. Within his own mind El Krunko had been taking a trip of his own, and the name of that trip was ass-kicking. Destination: Shakespeare. El Krunko knew that if they were going to make it through the Void he was going to have to pick up as much speed as he could muster. Faster and faster he full-throttled. The 2x4 burst into flame, not from wind resistance (as they were in a vacuum), but from the sheer power of the surf.

El Krunko cried out in agony, "Boots don't fail me now!"

While El Krunko was more concerned about breaking through the Void by breaking the light barrier, Happy continued to grunt, moan, and scream with the influx of this strange new power that was overtaking him. With a jolt, his muscles started increasing in size, until his shirt flew off, and his pants ripped from the rippling effect of his new Olympian stature. "AhhhhhhHH!!!!!!" Happy screamed. Waves of crackling electricity zipped and buzzed around his form, and sparked outward to surround the duo in a field of blue energy.

Being now completely encased in a Spiraling Electromagnetically Charged Happy Energy Vortex ™ El Krunko cried out in shock, "Without being able to see, there's no way we can get to light speed! We're doomed!"

Happy replied by screaming some more, and

soon, as they neared the Void slow enough that they were sure they were both going to be vaporized, they both fell silent.

The Vortex disappeared, and they found themselves standing upon an upward traveling escalator. Muzak played in the background. Vending machines occasionally passed by. An electronic voice was repeatedly welcoming them to the State of Og.

They curiously looked around, and found they were on one of a hundred thousand thousand escalators, all traveling upwards, and downwards, and sidewards, but all coalescing into a single point in the vast sky above.

"It.... all.... makes.... sense.... now!" Happy bellowed!

El Krunko scratched his head, and smacked Happy across the face."Daft Fool!" he declared.

But Happy had grown so immensely muscular that the slap ricocheted off unnoticed. Happy pointed toward their destination, and over the 20 minute waiting period it took for them to get there, explained their predicament.

"Don't you see! The strange Leprechaun warned me of this place! The Land of Og... It's a State of Mind! Literally! Once I finally remembered the mercenary assassin training of my past at Og Corp, I was able to put together the proper access code to allow us to travel here! At any time, no matter where in the multi-verse I might have been, once the, 'road-map' of my mind was written, I was pre-programmed to activate my return protocol and return here! Don't you see! I never completed my mission because of some strange amnesia, no doubt caused by Gribulor! Curse him! Somehow I ended up in that Time Capsule with you,

Ethnocentric Dracula and Miguel Sanchez Clone TK-421."

El Krunko nodded, munching on the innards of a vending machine he had decapitated. "What was your mission?"

Happy clenched his fists and gritted his teeth. "That's classified." El Krunko nodded and Happy continued. "Because of that amnesia, it was only a matter of time until the return protocols were activated in my mind, resulting in my eventual return to Og Corp, where I might receive my reward for the death of the Purple Aardvarks, and receive further missions." Happy smiled, and flexed all his muscles. "I will finally attain that which I've been struggling to be worthy of all these years. You, being Lord of the Slay, and my most esteemed associate and partner in intertimensional crime, may assist me in the great honor that will no doubt be bestowed upon me with my triumphant return."

"Wow." El Krunko burped as he finished his slushie. "Remembering your training sure made you fucking verbose."

Once the two of them finally reached the apex of the escalators, they stepped out onto the metal platform, and stretched their legs. A single hallway laid before them, and at the end of it was a neo-futuristically decorated foyer, fully stocked with bubble chairs, checkered carpets, paper-machet sculptures, a huge elevator bearing only the word, "OG." in large Courier Font, and a single button.

"What kind of rewards are we gonna get? Money?" El Krunko queried.

Happy pushed the button, and the two of them entered the elevator. "No, not money." Happy pressed for the lobby, and grinned viciously as the doors closed. "Ninja Training."

TABLET: CCV

The elevator doors opened. Another hallway stretched far before them. They strode down it, Happy smiling and confident, until they reached a door with a small gold plaque that read, "Dept. of Ninjology, and the Martial Arts."

Happy opened the door and peered inside. A large group of men, clothed in tight black jumpsuits, appeared interrupted... for they all stopped whatever they were doing, and swiftly turned and stood to attention, as alert as a room of ebony panthers. Eyes peered at the duo from behind black masks. Suddenly, without a noise from any of them, they attacked. Happy was crestfallen as he struggled to block the blows with his bare arms.

"We are betrayed!" El Krunko got mad, and reached for his trusty Ancestral Chainsaw, the action having become so much of a habit that he had momentarily forgotten it was gone! More ninja attacks ensued, with the pair slowly becoming overwhelmed. The flurry of blows impeded the slow manner in which they had to defeat their foes, and they gradually weakened. A laughing slowly became audible over the sounds of punching, kicking, and grasping.

"Know this, before you die! That all along it was Gribulor, the Great Goat-Man, triumphant!"

And lo, they learned the valuable lesson (which, thankfully, we in this advanced age have ensured every schoolchild learn), that it is Gribulor behind it all.

TABLET: CCVI

El Krunko stumbled backwards with each consecutive hit. As his strength began to wane, his arms flailed wildly, and his legs kicked in defiance. If he was to meet his most unfortunate and untimely demise at the hands of Gribulor's hench-ninja, he wasn't going to go down without a fight. Like a zebra stung by hundreds of rampaging scorpions, or a dolphin marauded by wild scallions, El Krunko spun in circles and made strange gurgling noises, while taunting the ninjii with rude gestures and foul smells. Clearly, if he was going to lose a battle, he was going to lose his mind first.

Happy, meanwhile, had backed himself into a corner, and stood helpless as he watched the death throes of his (now,) foul cohort. *This cannot be! The ninja of Og Corp are far too untrustworthy to be considered Gribulor's allies! They would never have betrayed their ancient oaths and joined Gribulor! They merely would have said they did, and then assassinated him at the drop of a chopstick!* Happy thought. And then he realized. These weren't ninja at all! They were mecha-ninja!

"Of course!" he screamed at the top of his lungs. Fourteen of the dark denizens encircled Happy, and carefully encroached upon his position. With each step they took closer to him, Happy hatched another segment of his plan... and then he launched it: projectile vomit that he'd been saving up from the trip through Garner-Vor. The grisly sight that ensued is far too hideous, even for those who now research such events lest they fail their Epic examinations. Merely know that a stench most horrid filled the room, and with it, sparks and smoke poured forth from every one of the mechanical monstrosities.

Happy stepped over their fallen foes, and wiped his chin clean on his sleeve.

El Krunko in a blind rage, was still struggling with their corpses.

"Goooooood. Goooood. You have proven yourself once more... Hero of legend." An elder voice spoke from the shadows.

The Olympian Happy turned, and soon found himself kneeling upon the ground as a sign of respect... for walking through the large bamboo doors on the opposite side of the room, was the single most feared martial artist in all the multi-verse.

Tales of his power had been chiseled on stone walls since the dawn of time. It was said he was older than the sun. His fingers were like daggers. His hands like axes. His arms were like swords, and his legs, spears. His whiskers were like chainsaws. His tail, a thunderbolt! And his breath... death. The eyes of this revered mouse master burned with the passion and wisdom of the ages, though his eyes were (of course), covered by a blindfold.

TABLET: CCVII

And so, many a month was spent by Happy and El Krunko in the tutelage of the great master, who was as nameless as he was deadly. When their time was over, the master spoke.

"And now... You are finally ready to fulfill your Epic destiny. Destroy Gribulor, and all shall be revealed!"

And so, they left.

Off they surfed towards the goat planet, but

along the way they spied–

* * * * * * * * * *

Happy, El Krunko, and Mestaphalm closed the ancient text. "That's it?" Happy cried. "But what about the ending?"

"How do you think I feel?" El Krunko said with a sigh.

Mestaphalm hushed his two companions.

"Quiet, or the evil guardians of this place will awaken, and surely Epic combat will ensue."

"Is THAT all? Well, why didn't you say so?" El Krunko replied, and let out a mighty bellow, one that vibrated both his vocal cords and the stone columns around them. Dust filled the air, let loose by the vibration. When El Krunko quieted, the chamber eerily silent. Then, off in the distance, there could be heard a low rumbling, slowly getting louder. El Krunko licked his lips and readied his Ancestral Chainsaw Mark IX. Happy unsheathed his giant sword, and Mestaphalm strung his magical bow with heat-seeking doom arrows.

"Get ready!" Mestaphalm screamed, for the noise had gotten almost deafening, and then from behind a column emerged the first of the guardians.

TABLET: CCVIII

With each lumbering step, the immense stone behemoth shook the ground, and with it dust and spackle fell from the vaulted crypt ceiling above them.

Happy and El Krunko lunged forward and met the beast in battle, while Mestaphalm let loose a mighty volley of arrows.

But it was to no avail.

They were soon all slain by the Unstoppable Indestructible Guardian Thing.

The End.

* * * * * * * * *

Rodney closed the most ancient text, and looked at his teacher bewildered. "Forgive me for my inquisitive ignorance, esteemed master. But it is most strange that the Legendary Heroes of the Green Pigs would be found in the lesser known Epic of Mestaphalm. I also find it even more confusing that they, who are said to be invincible, would find their demise at the maw of a lowly guardian."

Roger the Scholar nodded, and packed his pipe full with more tobacco. "Indeed. It is one of the great mysteries of the ages! Why would their end be chronicled in the pages of such pulp filth?"

Rodney shrugged. "I do not know, esteemed master, but if you forgive me for being so presumptuous with my assertions, I don't believe it's true. If they were all killed, then how did Mr. T, the author of Mestaphalm's Manifesto, truly know it had happened."

Roger smiled, and motioned for Rodney to follow him into his secret lair behind the wall of fishbowls. "It is now time for you to learn the truth, young Rodney. Come hither."

Eventually, they found themselves in the innermost sanctum of the temple... and there upon an altar most holy was a stone tablet. "Go to it, and read aloud the runes only scholarly masters must ever read," Roger said.

Rodney complied, and spoke loudly and clearly:

"El Krunko and Happy are dead. Whosoever who reads these words aloud is doomed to undertake the quest to bring them back to life, and solve the mystery of the ages."

With great pomp and circumstance, Rodney was ushered out of the temple, and into history.

After many years of questing, he found himself at the entrance of the great crypt of Mestaphalm.

TABLET: CCIX

"Finally, my years of questing are come to fruition!" he exclaimed happily. Rodney spoke the Great Words of Opening, "Great Words of Opening!" and the crypt door slid aside, slowly and deliberately, as if being pushed by one of great strength who still struggled a bit against the enormous weight. Rodney lit a torch and ventured inside.

Cobwebs lined the walls, upon which were carved an ancient pictographic text, with primitive drawings accompanying the even more primitive pictographs. Rodney peered closer, and found that the pictures depicted the most Epic moments available from the Epic selections of El Krunko's and Happy Barrypants' (or perhaps that should be Barry Happypants?) Epics.

There, before Rodney's eyes, were pictographs depicting their Epic struggle against the Elephant Man... the war with the Miguel Sanchii... the absurdity of the duo's time-traveling exploits... and others!

"Marvelous," Rodney whispered. "But a mere distraction." He traveled deeper into the crypt, and found himself in the main chamber, where before him were three large stone sarcophagi.

Upon each stood a carven statue of the great heroes: Happy and El Krunko, and the pulp hero, Mestaphalm.

Rodney set his satchel on the floor, and drew from it the elements needed for the resurrection ritual, on that he'd spent many years a-questing to obtain: eye of newt, dust from the floor of the Space-Caves of Gesperai, a dragon's egg, and Ramen noodles without the flavor packet.

Hours passed as the ritual was prepared. Finally, the elements were in their place, and Rodney opened the sarcophagi. He stood before them breathless, for inside were indeed the skeletons of the greatest heroes his world, or indeed any other world in the entire multi-verse, had ever known, and Mestaphalm's corpse too. Butterflies knotted in his stomach, and he struggled to regain his composure in view of these more-than-earthly remains.

TABLET: CCX

"Great Library of Tar'Bore protect my scholarly ways!" Rodney pulled the corpses from their ancient coffins, and lay them in the center of the summoning circle he had outlined on the stone ground. Hours of chanting ensued. Upon the last tonal inflection of the final syllable, an eerie mist rose up from the ground. Crackle! Snargle! Boom! Thunder filled the chamber, and as the mist dissipated with the cool draft... standing before the lowly Rodney were two of the most powerful entities he had ever read about, and Mestaphalm too, let's not forget about him.

Happy scratched his head and spun in circles. "The Guardian! It's gone!"

El Krunko instinctively reached for his A.C. Mark IX, but found it missing on his naked form. "My Ancestral Chainsaw! It's gone too!"

Mestaphalm's eyes narrowed, and his gaze locked upon Rodney, who was quivering with the excitement of unparalleled success.

"I resurrected you all!" Rodney cried out.

Happy cracked his knuckles. "To do your bidding, I presume."

Rodney shook his head and stood up. "Nay. I have brought you three back to life in order to solve the great mystery of the ages."

Mestaphalm began to sweat profusely, and very subtly he began to slink towards one of the stone statues.

Happy scratched his head once more (for it itched), and he pointed at Rodney with the other hand. "What mystery is that!?"

Rodney smiled. "The great mystery of the ages is as mysterious as it is great. I will ask, and you must answer."

El Krunko grinned broadly and took two steps forward. "Then ask, and we shall answer!"

Rodney raised his hands upon high and proclaimed, "Oh great legendary ones! Tell me this! Why were you in Mestaphalm's Epic?"

El Krunko and Happy looked to each other with dazed confusion. "Huh?"

And at that, Mestaphalm made his move.

He tore the stone sword from Happy's statue, and lunged at Rodney.

"I claim thy tale!"

With one clean stroke, Rodney's head was cut clean from his body. It landed upon the floor, and rolled up to El Krunko's feet. El Krunko's underpants was the last thing Rodney ever saw.

Mestaphalm laughed uncontrollably! "It is done! Now *I* have the power of authorship!"

Happy dropped to his knees and shook in sheer horror. "Noooooooooooooooo!!!!!!!!!!!!!!! Wait... What do you mean?!?" A low rumbling began to grow in the distance.

Mestaphalm turned to face them. "I knew Gribulor would never be able to defeat the two of you on your own grounds, so I tricked you into becoming part of my Epic! Then all I had to do was engineer our deaths, and create a secret cult that would perpetuate a false mystery, in order to create a new Epic. The Epic of he who would resurrect us from our untimely demise." The rumbling became louder. "And now that I have taken his head, I am outside of my own prior limitations! I am become Mestaphalm: Destroyer of Worlds!" Mestaphalm, the Destroyer of Worlds started rising into the air, with blue lightning bolts crackling off of his body.

As Happy cried over the loss, and as Mestaphalm continued his manic laughter, El Krunko's gaze turned to the severed head of Rodney... and it spoke to him. "El Krunko. You are our only hope. Before he gains his power, you must slay him."

El Krunko knew the proverb, "He who hesitates is tossed," and so he took Rodney's head from the ground, and hurled it into Mestaphalm with all his might. Boom! Blood and gore filled the room, and Mestaphalm, too, was no more.

But magic crackling blue light and energy continued to flood the chamber.

"Now what!?" Happy cried!

The Dynamic Duo backed up, and pressed their backs against the wall, and that's when they saw it... The world around them was beginning to deteriorate... vanishing into the void of nothingness.

"It's the end of the world.. AHHHHHH!HH! HH!!!?!?!?!"

TABLET: CCXI

Everything went white.

And stayed white.

All that was left, was Happy and El Krunko, floating naked in the white nothingness.

"Now what?" Happy cried in despair. "Everything's gone! And we, here, are the only things left in existence, forever! The horror, the horror!" Happy put his head into his hands and wept.

El Krunko, meanwhile, was lost in thought, his pointer finger and thumb slowly stroking his stubbly chin. The only sound he made was an extended and harmonious

"Hmmmmmmmmmmmmmmmmmmmmm..............
....."

El Krunko pondered over recent events, and wondered how he could possibly bring about the restoration of the world through Epic creation. Suddenly it came to him, and a light bulb appeared above his head, and became the first object to exist in the Universe, which should definitively answer the commonplace, yet still quizzically paradoxical question, "Which came first, the light bulb or the light?"

El Krunko opened his fanged mouth wide, and proclaimed, "Once upon a time..." and the white void was filled at dizzying speed with stars and planets, as if they burst forth from some reverse black hole, commonly referred to as a white hole, and upon the planets, at a speed so rapid that Happy and El Krunko's eyes could not take it all in, emerged flora and fauna. And the histories of all the beings of the Universe occurred before the hapless duo, and soon they even saw themselves repeat their Epic deeds. Happy slapped himself in the forehead at his most foolish actions, but El Krunko had a good laugh while reviewing his exploits.

Suddenly they were bodily swept up into the twirling, whirling void of creation, and everything once more was still, or should I say time flowed once more at its standard pace. They found themselves surfing towards the goat planet, on their proscribed quest to defeat the evil Gribulor, when Happy spied something out of the corner of his eye.

"Look!" he marveled to El Krunko, and pointed to a sector of space.

TABLET: CCXII

* * * * * * * * * *

Happy, El Krunko, and Mestaphalm closed the ancient text. "That's it?" Happy cried. "But what about the ending?"

"How do you think I feel?" El Krunko said with a sigh.

Mestaphalm hushed his two companions.

"Quiet, or the evil guardians of this place will awaken, and surely Epic combat will ensue."

El Krunko was just about to give out the

mightiest of mighty bellows, when suddenly and mysteriously his mind became awash with the information of his past (or should I say future?) exploits.

With a vicious grin, El Krunko wielded his Ancestral Chainsaw Mark IX, and chopped Mestaphalm into little itty bits. Happy merely watched, bewildered, as El Krunko reduced even the skeleton of Mestaphalm into dust, then snorted every last spec of it.

After the deed was done, he took Happy's head clean off, and followed it up with cutting his own head from his body. Sure enough, they re-awoke years later in a summoning circle, with Rodney standing before them.

"I resurrected you both!" Rodney proclaimed smiling.

El Krunko leapt forward, and was about to chop Rodney's head off, and claim the tale as his, but alas, "My Ancestral Chainsaw! It's Gone! Dammit!"

Rodney was about to continue with asking his question, to which there must be an answer, but El Krunko had no time for chit-chat. Instead he tackled Rodney to the ground, and hog-tied him with cloth he tore from his clothes.

Happy scratched his head, true to form, and queried, "Umm... ?"

El Krunko laughed insidiously and pressed his foot down hard upon Rodney's chest. "Happy, there's only one way we can regain that which is rightfully ours." With hand gestures he explained his plan, and with great protest from Rodney, in the form of muffled grunts, the Dynamic Duo slew Rodney together, hand in hand.

TABLET: CCXIII

* * * * * * * * * *

The Epic of Happy Barrypants and El Krunko, Or, Conversely, The Epic of El Krunko and Happy Barrypants

El Krunko held him down, while Happy grasped Rodney's head in his hands. He placed his feet on Rodney's shoulders, and pulled his head clean off with a crunch and a rip.

And now, the pair were forever locked together in Epic-ness, and this entire Epic must now be renamed, "The Epic of Happy Barrypants and El Krunko, Or, Conversely, The Epic of El Krunko and Happy Barrypants."

The pair exited the crypt, and found themselves in a quaint mountain village. In order to work out the kinks in their recently resurrected muscles, they quickly razed the town, slaying its inhabitants and buggering the sheep. "Ah," El Krunko said. "Its good to be back."

They rested briefly before and continuing on their way.

But what was this?!

A vicious, two headed serpent!

They slew it.

Behold! A monstrous, three-toed sloth!

It met the fate of the serpent.

Egads! A flock of giant, screeching, razor-taloned falcons!

Quick work was made of them.

Sacre bleu! A man made of fire!

His life was extinguished.

Zounds! A learned scholar, dressed in robes!

"What the hell is going on here?" El Krunko demanded of the man. "Our Epic seems caught in random encounter mode!"

The scholar sighed, and nodded, and said, "You speak the truth, Lord of the Slay."

TABLET: CCXIV

"You want the truth!?" El Krunko boasted. "You can't handle the truth!"

The scholar sadly agreed that he could not, and short work was made of him.

For hours upon hours, the Dynamic Duo tromped down the mountain path, turning it into barren wasteland as they inched from random battle to random battle. Finally, weary and covered head to toe in blood and ichor, but feeling a few levels higher than before, the two collapsed at the foothills of an even greater mountain range.

"Pant. Pant. I can't go on El Krunko! I must rest." Happy rolled over and fell asleep in his own filth. El Krunko was a kind and patient man, but he wouldn't have any slouching on behalf of his Epic partner. After a moments rest, El Krunko took Happy upon his own shoulders, and continued slaughtering mercilessly all through the night.

When Happy awoke, he was somewhat surprised to see they were in the center of an immense palace. Columns of ivory, fine silk tapestries, and furniture of jade and gold adorned the exquisitely beautiful throne room. El Krunko was snoring loudly atop a most high column of corpses. Happy stood up, and shook the tiredness from his bones. He awoke his ally, and heard many a wondrous tale of all the sights and slayings he had missed during his slumber.

As El Krunko was getting to the best part, about how the last town he razed was populated with only midget women and children, the wall behind the throne exploded outward, littering the chamber in brick and rock. Standing before them were two barbarians of fearsome stature. One wielded a sword bigger than a Snar Dragon, and the other a gargantuan double-bladed axe.

Happy fell backwards and cried aloud, "Noooo! It can't be! Conan El King and Kull El Conqueror! Noooo!"

TABLET: CCXV

"The very same!" the two replied in unison. Then, with a swish and whirl, they brandished their weapons. "We have no idea who you are, so you must be puny nothing-beings!" said both together, creating an eerie echo. "We shall smite you as we have half this world!" And it was true, C.E.K. and K.E.C. had indeed slain half the inhabitants of the world, just as El Krunko and Happy had been murdering the other half. The four were the only beings left alive on the entire planet. And now they clashed in armed combat!

"Fools!" El Krunko cried. "I am El Krunko, and this be my Epic!"

The powerful beings struggled, punching and kicking and blocking and dodging and grasping and hitting and wrestling and head butting and elbowing and kneeing and rolling about. But it seemed to be to no avail, as no advantage could be gained on either side.

Could it be that each duo had finally met its

match?

Fear not, silly reader. The battle was long, but El Krunko and Happy triumphed.

They seized their opponents weapons, and sent C.E.K. and K.E.C. running to the hills.

TABLET: CCXVI

Overcome with joy because of their magnificently triumphant victory, our euphoric heroes started jumping up and down in an idiotic display of happiness. "Hooray!!" Happy cried aloud as he hopped around the throne room.

"We did it!" El Krunko, caught up in the same mindless glee (which could only be explained by the fact the barbarian buddies Conan and Kull were overly fond of head butts), challenged Happy to a jumping contest, and soon they were leaping so high, and so hard, that the ceiling collapsed, and the room quickly became a courtyard.

Higher, and higher they bounced into the stratosphere. At the apex of his most powerful jump, El Krunko declared himself the winner, and changed the challenge into a diving contest.

Down, down they dove. Spins galore! Jackknives a plenty! Clotheslines and claws abound!

"The Dominator!" Happy screamed, and he flew through the air, smashing into El Krunko with all his might.

"The Jackhammer!" El Krunko back flipped through the sky, then dropped his feet into Happy's groin as he fell.

"THE CANNONBALL!" They both screamed at the top of their lungs, and smashed into the planets surface. The palace they had recently acquired was supremely detonated in the obliterating blow, and in the colossal collision, the Dynamic Duo careened deep into... the hidden underground civilization of the monkeys!

TABLET: CCXVII

"Ugh." El Krunko groaned as he arose.

"My head hurts!" Happy moaned. El Krunko's eyes slowly re-focused, and he gasped.

All around him were tiny monkeys, brandishing spears that were like forks to the pair, with large iron helmets.

"Awwww..." El Krunko cooed. "Look at all the cute little monkeys!" With a hollering and a screeching, the monkeys lunged at the pair, climbing up their bodies to attack them, only to leap away, making them really extra annoying.

"Ack!" El Krunko's opinion had rapidly changed. "You little bastards!"

Happy swung his arms out, and a group of the small primates flew across the battle field, some never to breathe the cool air of their home world again. But there were too many. Happy and El Krunko ran away, thrashing away at the monkeys that followed as rapidly as they could run.

BOOM! Happy had run straight into traffic in the middle of Great Ape Avenue, and a yellow cab had struck him squarely. The automobile crumpled, and Happy's balance momentarily faltered. When he regained it he looked around, and was amazed.

They were in the midst of a massive monkey metropolis!

TABLET: CCXVIII

The vaulted cavernous ceiling was outstretched hundreds of feet above them, and they could see no end to the urban sprawl in every direction they turned. Tens of thousands of trees littered the city, all of which rose high into the air. Between, amidst, among, and around the trees were bridges, houses, tents, workshops, and buildings of every shape and design imaginable... And populating the city were a seemingly endless supply of monkeys of all shapes and sizes. Every few blocks were hot air balloons of monkeys floating in the sky, with large glowing lanterns hung from them by ropes, all illuminating the maze of street work beneath them. Honks and horns a plenty surrounded the duo, and monkeys began to accost them, as their presence in the middle of the street were keeping them from their monkey business.

Monkeys with spears tackled the pair while they were awestruck by the monktropolis, and they quickly found themselves shackled and chained by the monkey militia. El Krunko and Happy were lifted into the air, and carried down Great Ape Ave, taking a quick left onto Banana Boulevard, before finally arriving at Chimpanzee Central Circle.

Out heroes were set down in the middle of the parking lot, while monkeys with balloons tied to their tails flew up to them. Their yellow hats said, "Press," and they scribbled fastidiously in their notebooks with crayons.

After being interviewed at great length, Happy and El Krunko overheard that the Mayor of the city was on his way there to inspect the prisoners. They further went on to discover that he was not just the Mayor, but was also running for Governor in the next election with a healthy lead in the polls, all of which was just a political stepping stone for him becoming Emperor of the whole civilization.

Happy shook with terror, while El Krunko wrote a speech announcing his candidacy to run for Mayor.

TABLET: CCXIX

Soon the Mayor, the Honorable Good Good Gorilla Guy arrived. He stood an imposing three feet tall, with a fancy silk cape, and fur as red as brick. He examined the prisoners. Happy, upon seeing him, exclaimed, "A Red Monkey! Are you a prophesier?"

The Mayor glared at Happy with his beady eyes, and sniffed him. "Ooo-aah boogly gabbah goo heee heee gabble!" he exclaimed, and the monkeys let them loose.

"Welcome to my land!" the Mayor proudly exclaimed, whereupon he led them back to their overworld palace, apologizing for their treatment along the way. El Krunko was mollified, for the time at least, by Good Good Gorilla Guy's superb manners (he had, after all, attended Madame Baboon's premier finishing school). That, and the fact that he had a fetish for Red Monkey women, and spied a few choice specimens strolling along the roads on the way.

A large retinue followed them, and once the surface was reached, quickly set to work on repairing the palace. Paws clawed telephones, and in came electrician gibbons, carpenter apes, and mason monkeys. Shrill cries and high pitched chirping filled the chambers, nearly drowning out the words spoken between our heroes and the Mayor.

Good Good Gorilla Guy proposed to them a plan, where Happy and El Krunko, who were already gaining notoriety in the liberal chimp-owned media, would publicly support his election for Governor and campaign for Emperor. In exchange, Good Good Gorilla Guy promised our Dynamic Duo consulting jobs, with lucrative stock options and high yield bonds. Happy, with dreams of diamonds and gold on his mind, heartily agreed to the proposition. El Krunko was anxious to go bar hopping in search of some Red Monkey tail, and agreed merely to wrap the conversation up.

And so the plan was hatched...

TABLET: CCXX

El Krunko was halfway back to the hole, when his associates stopped him. Happy and Good Good Gorilla Guy were not so eager to leave just yet, and wanted to celebrate tea time. El Krunko begrudgingly grabbed a six pack from the fridge and started pre-gaming.

And so, as the repairs went on around them, Happy, El Krunko, and G.G.G.G. sat down for a chat over tea and crumpets.

"So, tell me..." G.G.G.G. queried as he leaned back and stroked his beard, "What are two upstanding gentlemen, as powerful, and as cunning as yourselves, doing here?" He gestured around at the ruins of the grand palace. "Surely this marvelous marble structure was once the prime center of the surface barbarians' civilization." He took a sip of his tea with his pinky politely extended. "It surely could not have been an easy task for you both to come by its acquisition."

El Krunko leaned forward and smiled. "It was nothin'. Really. And neither was wiping out their entire puny race. I don't even know where *here* is! We never really figured that part out. And you know what... I don't care."

"But I do," said G.G.G.G.

And so, late through the night, and into the early morning, El Krunko and Happy recited their Epics. G.G.G.G. was astonished. If these two were truly as amazing as they had described, with a little bit of manipulation, and a plethora of his diabolical dastardliness, he would be able to utilize them as pawns in his grandiose scheme that had been baking in his mind since he was but a child. He stood up, and led our heroes into the garden outside the palace (which was nearly fixed).

"You see that planet up there." And G.G.G.G. pointed up into the atmosphere. The duo looked, and sure enough a massive green orb was in orbit high above them.

"Yeah, so?" they both shrugged.

"Well," he continued, "it's mine. And it just so happens that it follows me wherever I go. How about if after we win the elections–"

Happy shuddered, and El Krunko gasped for joy. "I see where you're going with this!" the Lord of the Slay happily exclaimed. "We move the entire civilization of monkeys onto your planet, and then we can go traveling with our ape army, gorilla goons, and monkey marauders, to take over other planets, just like I did with Trunk! It's bloody–"

"Brilliant." G.G.G.G. calmly replied. "Yes, yes, I know. Your Epics made me think of it. That's why I'm going to make you two *full* partners."

And so, the Dynamic Duo was no more, and the Triumphant Trio agreed to work together.

They ventured back into the underground to enact their takeover of the monkey world.

It should be known, however, that Good Good Gorilla Guy was not as honorable as he seemed, and who knows what dark and mysterious plans he had up his sleeves?

Had Happy and El Krunko walked into a trap?

Was this Gribulor's doing, as all school children would suspect?

Were they doomed to death at the hands of this strange supervillain?

Dun Dun Dun...

TABLET: CCXXI

And then it happened.

El Krunko's third eye opened.

He bashed down the 4th wall.

IT WAS GRIBULOR'S DOING!

El Krunko grabbed his Ancestral d20 and rolled. 20! Plus his 8,000 point Lord of the Slay bonus. El Krunko successfully disbelieved the illusion.

Suddenly, El Krunko found himself floating in a barrel of pickled pork rinds. El Krunko's eyes were set ablaze with inner fire. Enraged, he exploded out of the barrel. Happy came tumbling alongside him, who was scratched his head as he wondered what the hell had just happened.

Gribulor stood before the two at the console of a mammoth computer. He laughed maniacally and pulled a giant lever.

El Krunko screamed out, "I'm tired of the Epics

taking needlessly wandering plot twists! THIS ENDS NOW GRIBULOR!"

Eyes still ablaze; mullet under kerchief rustling in the wind from an unseen source; progressive guitar solo playing in the background; El Krunko Powered Up. His goatee glowed gold and grew longer than even ZZ Top could imagine.

"Heba-Meba-Jeba-Cow!" El Krunko uttered the magic words again and again, and he started gaining new powers increasing at a stupefying rate. Four arms exploded from his sides. His skin became forged of golem skin. A twenty barreled rat cannon exploded from his chest and fired starving rodents onto Gribulor, whereupon they ate him alive. El Krunko's eyes were lasers. His fingernails grew eight feet. An army of Chewbaccas belched from his maw. Toxic storm brew from his arse.

Drunk with power, El Krunko continued to sing the words, and his power continued to grow without check. Dimensions were crossed. All Epics were becoming Krunko. All video games based on Epics were morphing so that Krunko was both hero and villain simultaneously. The hearts and minds of everyone everywhere were ultimately falling prey to the seemingly invincible will of the Krunk. His control over the Universe was increasing at a rate that grew so fast it could not be perceived. There was no stopping the Power Bloated Krunkian Menace. Hope faded from the galaxy.

TABLET: CCXXII

El Krunko started suddenly in his chair. He had fallen asleep to the sweet sweet sound of fine monkey craftsmanship going on around him. Happy and that Great Great Good Good Gorilla Guy were nowhere to be seen.

But El Krunko was disturbed by his dream.

Could it have been a vision of the future?

Dun Dun Dun...

TABLET: CCXXIII

El Krunko wandered through the ancient halls of the former Barbarian King's stronghold, dazed and mystified by his fanciful daydreamed delusion. Stopping only to briefly command the monkey workers to construct parapets here, turrets there, and portcullis a plenty, he continued to make his way deep into the bowels of the Dreary Dungeon ™. Deeper he drudged down, through the labyrinth of levels overflowing with slimes, oozes, and a multiples of minotaurs. Lost in thought, contemplating his predicament, the idea of combat with any of them never even occurred to him.

Eventually, El Krunko's mindless meanderings brought him at last to the Great Lost Library of Tar'Bore. Tens of thousands of ancient texts, scrolls, tablets, books, codices, and tomes were at his disposal. El Krunko passed them all by, as a child would a broccoli bar. But, when El Krunko brushed past one of the larger shelves, a twinkling glint caught his eye. There, placed upon its ivory altar, were the Renowned Glasses of Nerdliness, second only in intellectual offerings to the Great Monocle of Genius that El Krunko had briefly possessed in his scholarly days.

El Krunko knelt beside the altar, and weighed the issue carefully before him. "Once I've thought to my thoughts content," he said to himself. "I could always taken them off when I'm finished... That way no one would know the secret nerdly heritage of my ideas."

Settling the matter, he picked the holy relic up donned the glasses. El Krunko's bloody rags transformed into trousers and a button down shirt. His marvelous mullet was downsized into a fair fro. A pocket protector replaced his scalp collection. And best of all (for it amounted at a gain rather than a loss), his empty Ancestral Chainsaw hanger, was transformed into an Ancestral Calculator. El Krunko had become Professor El Krunko: Lord of the Sagely Slay. Whipping out his A.C. he did some quick calculations, carried the remainders, and formulated a plan. With pristine precision he absorbed the knowledge of the, "P," section of the library, and in the matter of a half hour, awarded himself full PhD.'s in Psychology, Philosophy, Planning, Power, and Popcorn.

Snacking on the fruit of his success, El Krunko entered the world of interior monologue.

"Psychology tells me that I dreamed of fighting Gribulor, the Great Goat-Man. I don't even know him... He's Happy's arch-nemesis. My counterpart from the future couldn't defeat him because Happy was dead. If Happy died in the future, and it was his Epic at the time, then no wonder my alternate couldn't win! He was confronted with someone else's arch-nemesis, and had no arch-ally to combat him. Right now, my exploits are shared equally with Happy, as this Epic belongs to both of us. If I could somehow get rid of Gribulor now, while I still have the chance, then Happy would no longer serve any purpose to me. When I dreamt of killing Gribulor, it must have meant that my unconscious yearned for Happy's demise. In my own

Epic, the Quest o' Matic 5000 tasked me with taking over the Universe in my own dreams. Right now Shakespeare is all that's preventing me from doing just that."

"Philosophy tells me that reality is made manifest through actions I take in my dreams."

"Planning tells me that if I kill Shakespeare, and take over the Universe in my dreams, then I could kill Gribulor in reality, finally get rid of Happy once and for all. Then the Epic will be mine again!"

"Power tells me that an Epic is the most powerful form of existence in the multi-verse. Everything exists. If an Epic contains everything, then it must exist supreme! Therefore, the purpose of an Epic is to take over other Epics! Therefore, in order for me to gain ultimate power, my Epic must rule supreme! To do just that, I must take over all the other Epics that ever existed! If a whole civilization's legacy existed only in written slabs of knowledge, then if I destroyed that knowledge, it would no longer exist... except as a mere footnote in *my* Epic, made greater by their destruction! Of course! The truth of the Universe and supreme power is at my grasp!"

"Popcorn tells me nothing."

El Krunko promptly ripped up his Popcorn PhD, as he found it useless, and set about burning the library to the ground. In a matter of minutes, the Great Lost Library of Tar'Bore, and its collections of a thousand learned races was destroyed. An irreplaceable wealth of information concerning only the matters of galactic peace and prosperity had perished. It's endless supply of knowledge, wisdom, and lore, was turned to ashes.

El Krunko laughed hysterically.

TABLET: CCXXIV

El Krunko tossed the glasses into the fire, their dorky power no longer of use to him. They cracked and melted, and El Krunko strode out of the burning library, confident in his new-found knowledge.

Meanwhile, the election campaign was on!

"These two gentlemen are great intergalactic heroes," Good Good Gorilla Guy spoke into the microphone. "And they've come here to endorse my candidacy for Governor! Isn't that right?"

Happy nodded, and the great throng of monkeys and apes that had gathered to hear the eloquent orator G.G.G.G. roared and cheered.

"And when I am elected, the monkey planet will know the greatness that it has long deserved!"

A massive cheer went up again, and the monkeys raised their banners, upon which were written, "Gorilla Guy in '117!" and, "Good Good Gorilla Guy is great!" The crowd was putty in G.G.G.G.'s hands, and he molded them as he saw fit, into a lean, mean, voting constituency.

A few weeks later, the polls were in, and G.G.G.G. was elected by a landslide! He overwhelmed the polls with an overwhelming majority over his opponent, Overwhelmingly Okay Orangutan.

El Krunko was elated when he heard the results. Now all he had to do wait until G.G.G.G. was crowned Emperor, and him to attack the planet of the Goat-Men, so that Gribulor could be slain, and El Krunko could be one step closer to absolute power!

But G.G.G.G. had other plans...

TABLET: CCXXV

And so, after the induction ceremony, the Triumphant Trio retired to the Governor's mansion, where could be discussed the future of Monktropolis, the most populated of the four cities in this, the great lost monkey civilization of Tar'Bore.

Everyone was in attendance! It was a fine soiree' of all the celebrities and big whigs in monkey high society. There was Arnold Chimpenator, Chimp Woolery, Richard Gibbons, Tony Shalhoub, the award winning star of Monkey, Grape Ape, Mallard the Duck (a foreigner), and a slew of other famous socialites. El Krunko and Happy were dressed in tuxedos of the finest caliber, while G.G.G.G. had donned the Governors hat (a purple tophat), and was parading around in his finest silks, beating away the paparazzi with a Gucci shillelagh.

At the climax of the party, El Krunko was appointed Mayor of Monktropolis, to which he exclaimed, "I hereby rename the city, Krunktropolis." And there was much rejoicing.

Once many of the guests had left, the Joint Chiefs of State, Governor Good Good Gorilla Guy, and Happy, attended a secret meeting without Mayor El Krunko.

While the minutes of the mysterious meeting are lost to time, it is commonly accepted that they planned the events which proceeded over the course of the next several weeks. Suffice to say, the end result was the secession of Krunktropolis from the rest of the Monkey Union. Once free of his former political bindings, G.G.G.G. Declared war against the remaining three states, claiming that the war would end, only when the other Governor's capitulated to G.G.G.G.G.'s superiority, and accepted his rise to Supreme Emperor.

Mayor El Krunko paraded the streets rallying monkeys to war. He single-handedly trained hoards of them into a lean, mean, well-trained army.

Meanwhile, unbeknownst to the Mayor, Happy was arrested by agents of the M.I.A. (Monkey Intelligence Agency), and was smuggled into the deep dark clutches of Grey Gorilla Ville, to the west.

TABLET: CCXXVI

And so, by means of coercion so secretive that even I, the Author, do not know, Happy forced into the service of the Grey Gorilla Ville Villains, and he too trained an army, one as powerful, ruthless, and cunning as that of Mayor El Krunko's army of monkeys in Krunktropolis.

The Epic war that spanned the next few centuries is chronicled in the great poet Homonker's grand narrative poem, "The Apiad," and need not be recounted here. One can easily refer to that work by visiting the local library. And as that work will tell, "Twas no soul whose life went unchanged, no family whose kin were left unaffected by the bloody slaughter, no shortage of tragic love stories, and no atrocity that went uncommitted, for *that* war consumed the entire monkey civilization, as well as a dozen other neighboring civilizations on nearby stars as well.

The entire mess finally ended when Happy realized that his Epic companion, Mayor El Krunko, was on the other side fighting against him the entire time! Happy quickly came to the side of his ally, and massacred the descendants of the very army he had helped train.

And when it was all over, and many cities had been reduced to rubble, and many billions had died, and the entire Black Badger species of Sirus 11 were extinct, Mayor El Krunko, Happy, and G.G.G.G.G. stood triumphant, but bloodied.

"Mwa hahahahahaha HAHAHAHA!" G.G.G.G.G. laughed a laugh of pure bile and hatred.

Mayor El Krunko was taken aback. "You know, you're not really that good... in fact... You're kinda mean," he noted.

Governor Good Good Gorilla Guy suddenly shrunk back, as if someone had struck him. "What?! How do you... uh, nothing, nothing."

Mayor El Krunko found the monkey's reaction strange, and scratched his chin. "Hmmmmm...."

That night, at the victory celebration, Mayor El Krunko was nowhere to be seen... That is, of course, unless you looked for him scaling the side of the Chimperial Palace, straight towards G.G.G.G.G.'s office window!

TABLET: CCXXVII

Mayor El Krunko heard the sound of voices from high above, and soon he was perched like the ninja he was, against the cold hard stone, hanging by only his ninja desire to not fall.

"Yes, oh lord, I will obey," a monkey chimed from within the room.

That's the voice of the three banana General! he thought.

"Mwa hahahahahaha. Then they shall be destroyed!" an unfamiliar voice boomed. "Go now!

Leave me, and do my bidding of doom and manipulative mayhem."

"Yes, Supreme Emperor Elect, I will obey... and DESTROY!"

Footsteps sounded out, followed by the slamming of a door.

"Eeep eeeep eeeeeeeeeeep!!!!!" screeched a female.

"Eeeeeep eeep eeep eeep!" cried another female.

"Eeeeeekek eeep eeeep!" squealed another.

"*What the? I know those shrieks!* thought Mayor El Krunko, as he gritted his teeth, and made his best attempt to stay quiet, lest his position be noticed. *Tis the newly formed Mayoral Concubine Squad that I created nearly a decade ago. Zounds! What are they doing here?*" He tightened his ninja grip, and ninja listened more intently.

"You are probably wondering why I have summoned you all here."

"Eeeep eeekkkkkkk!" they howled.

"As you know, I am now the most powerful monkey of all, the Monkey Supreme, if you will. And it is time that my official plans for the crowning of the planet that follows me around, and, until now, remained nameless, as the Super Space Monkey Capital of the Galaxy!"

The M.C.S. hollered, howled, and roared with approval.

"I will offer each of you a hundred thousand dukats, and a lifetime supply of bananas and cigarettes if you work for me, secretly spying on Mayor El Krunko. As you know, he has been battle worn, and I fear that he may try to usurp my power. Do everything he says, and remember! If he's harmed in any way, you shall be destroyed... He is, after all, still the Mayor. But always report back to me."

"Eeep eeep!" They agreed!!!

El Krunko leapt through the window, shattering it apart with his mighty thigh muscles, and landed, ninja swords and throwing stars a-flyin' through the air, until the M.C.S. was filleted into a pile of raunchy, flesh seared, goo.

Governor Good Good Gorilla Guy stepped back, and gasped a forcefully feigned and badly acted shock of surprise (since he had known El Krunko was there all along)!

"Jeepers. It's the Mayor."

TABLET: CCXXVIII

"Ah ha!" Mayor El Krunko cried out. "Now I know *all* about your secret plan, to discover my secret plan!"

"So..." G.G.G.G.G. stood and faced his opponent head on. "You admit then, that you've been planning on usurping my throne, and taking it for yourself, do you?" G.G.G.G.G. disapproved.

"Well, uh…" Mayor El Krunko was confused. The thought *occasionally* came to mind, it's true, but he never actually took any steps towards performing a coup, much less work out the details of such a plan. Although, let's face it here folks, El Krunko doesn't plan much of anything, preferring to blindly leap into a situation and hope his Epic prowess will be enough to see him out of said situation alive. Like the situation he's now found himself in, caught up on the very trip wires of his own impulsiveness!

"If you want to get technical," Mayor El Krunko attempted to reassert himself, "I had never really gotten to the planning stage, per se…"

"Ah ha! So you admit to having thought about thinking about a plan to usurp my throne!"

Mayor El Krunko couldn't deny it, for he always told the truth.

"Very well then, El Krunko," G.G.G.G.G. replied to his admission. "I appreciate you telling the truth. And since your Epic prowess did help me win this war, and take over the entirety of the monkey civilization, I merely strip you of your Mayorship, and sentence you to exile. Now be gone."

"Whew!" El Krunko sighed in relief. Grabbing a pane of glass he found nearby from his premature entrance into the office, he surfed off, seeking his true friend and ally, Happy Barrypants. And soon he spied him below, still in the midst of the post-war celebration, inebriated more than El Krunko had ever seen him, and necking an orangutan woman.

"C'mon!" El Krunko said, lifting Happy up by the seat of his pants. "Let's go." And with Happy in his arms, he surfed off into the cosmos.

"What gives?" Happy slurred. "I was gonna score with that chimp."

"First of all, she was an orangutan. And secondly, there are better looking apes out there. Trust me, I know." Which was true, for during the long war El Krunko had many chances to sate his lust for primate flesh.

And so they soared, until they reached edge of space, and lo they found a strange sight, an ancient, white bearded man sitting at a writing desk, while floating through space. He was scribbling away with quill on parchment. Their curiosity was piqued, and El Krunko surfed over to the man.

"Hail! What manner of being art thou, that can withstand the cold vacuum of space in nothing more than tattered robes, and maintain the composure to write as if nothing fazed him?" El Krunko was surprised at the eloquence he suddenly possessed.

"Your newly-found eloquence is my doing, El Krunko," replied the hoary septuagenarian without looking up from his page, "as is your presence here, at the very ends of the Universe. For I am The Author!"

TABLET: CCXXIX

"Of what?" Happy retorted, drunk beyond words, yet using them all the same.

"Why of all of creation of course," he softly replied.

"Ohhhhhhh.... that. Never read it!" Happy oinked. "You know. Books and all."

El Krunko stood aghast. Could this possibly be true? Had the Bronze Tablet of The Epic of Liu Bei been telling the truth? Were all Epics created by the same insidious and manipulative consciousness? Was there really a big Epic Game going on? Was he, and all the other Epic Personas just pawns on the same diabolical playing field for a single mastermind's solitary insidious purpose?

"Fuck that! Free will bitch!" El Krunko yelled aloud in defiance, and he furiously leapt forward while reaching for his Ancestral Chainsaw... but alas! "Tis gone like the shadows of the misty morning haze in the dawn of a spring day. What a curious situation I seem to have been inadvertently thrust in. A pox on my reluctance to hesitate!" El Krunko scratched his chin, and pondered aloud. "By Job! What am I saying?"

The Author leaned forward, and gazed at his bewildered buddy. "A mere demonstration my young lad. I can make you say anything I want... for I am The Author."

Happy pushed El Krunko aside, and stepped forward. "Ok mac. You obviously have something to tell us, so spit it out. I've got primates to get primal with, and I'm losin' my buzz."

El Krunko agreed to hear the scholarly man out, and so, upon a nearby water planet, the three of them set down on a small island, and had a chat of most Epic proportions.

"You see," The Author began, "you are both Epic, and are therefore in the Game."

"And what game is that?" El Krunko hastily replied.

"The Epic Game. As you already know, El Krunko, the purpose of all Epics are to destroy other Epics. What you *don't* know, is that in order to qualify for the final round, your Epic must meet some prerequisite requirements, which at the moment, it does not."

Happy threw El Krunko a harsh look, and the Lord of the Slay merely averted his gaze, and looked as innocent as possible.

"In order to qualify, all submitted Epics must have a beginning, and they must also be unfinished. Epics with endings are inadmissable, and are considered to have been eaten by other Epics. All Epics must invoke the muses. They must have a proper Title... And they must have only *one* character. In the end... There can be only one."

El Krunko leaned forward, and softly spoke... "One Epic... or one Epic Character?"

"Both!" The Author frabjously declared.

"Die fiend! Taste wretched wretchedness!" The Dynamic Duo screamed together at the top of their lungs... and they lunged at each other, grasping at their throats, and clawing at the other's eyes.

"Stop this madness!" The Author proclaimed, and indeed, the two found themselves politely apologizing. "As I was about to say, the two of you are currently the best candidates for making it to the, 'Playoffs,' as it were, but unless you work together, you will *both* find yourselves lacking an Epic that meets the requirements, in order to ultimately meet each other in final death defying conflict over the grand prize..."

The Author sighed, and wrote himself a cold beverage while Happy and El Krunko mulled over his words. Finally, The Author shook his head, and gave each of them a disappointed look. "Neither of you have even bothered to invoke the muses, and that's the easiest part!" Happy and El Krunko sunk their heads, both ashamed of their poor study habits.

"But still..." El Krunko said as a smile returned to his face. "You gotta admit, all things taken into consideration, we were doing pretty well for ourselves..." He looked to The Author's face for approval, but found none given. "Right?

The Author shook his head as solemnly as a mortician. "The two of you are but a stone's throw from defeat."

It was Happy's turn to speak up. "No way! We totally won that war, and I was about to get lucky! I'd say *I* was doing a pretty damn good job, if I do say so myself."

The Author closed his eyes, and sighed. "The evil overlord of the Great Monkey Civilization has been plotting, all this time, to usurp the very Epic the two of you find yourselves now in."

"What do you mean?" El Krunko questioned. "We left Supreme Emperor Elect Governor Good Good Gorilla Guy in charge of the whole thing, and you're not gonna tell me that some good schmo is gonna to take both of us on."

"Silly El Krunko." The Author smiled. "You have been deceived. Governor Good Good Gorilla Guy is no more than Former-Mayor Mean Mean Monkey Man, and with his infernal lust for power, and his enormous super monkey intelligence, he has prepared to go back in Epic Time, and take over complete control."

"Oh my God! The horror!" Happy sobbed. El Krunko's cheeks turned red at the thought of making such a blatant error.

"You must go now, and prevent him from taking that which you have worked so long to achieve... and remember. You can never erase the Epic Text... You can only add to it!"

And so, the Dynamic Duo rose, and pledged to solve this dilemma most bewildering, and restore balance to the Epic-verse.

"But wait...? Why are you helping us?" El Krunko asked, suddenly confused, as if the entire discussion with this mysterious stranger who called himself The Author had left him with more questions, and only half-answers, that didn't help very much.

"Because..." The Author answered...

TABLET: CCXXX

"I have grown Epically old, older than either of you could possible imagine, and my time is coming to an end. Which is why the final winning Epic must be chosen soon! For if it is not, and I find myself writing the final line of my existence, than the entire space-time continuum would be thrown into disarray! Now go, and achieve your Epic fate!" And with that, he disappeared.

El Krunko and Happy raced back to the ape planet, anxious to stop Mean Mean Monkey Man's malicious monkey business. They burst through the stained glass window of the Chimperial Palace Throne Room, where they spied the dastardly villain climbing into the driver's seat of a vintage automobile.

"Stop, fiend!" El Krunko cried, but it was too late. The car sped off and disappeared.

Happy leapt down and grabbed the cuff of M.M.M.M.'s chief advisor, Orangutan Stan, and lifted him into the air. "Where has he gone, you hairy ape?"

"Thanks for the compliment, but you can't stop him! Soon all of this will be his, and I will be right hand ape to the most powerful being in the Universe!"

But that was not to be, for Happy tore the ape apart with his bare hands in a rage. "What now?" he asked El Krunko.

El Krunko shrugged, and looked around the chamber for a clue, anything to give some indication of where M.M.M.M. had gone, but when he turned back to Happy, his ally had dropped to the floor, dead!

"Egads!" El Krunko gasped. "We're already too late!"

TABLET: CCXXXI

The Lord of the Slay fell to his knees, and cradled his dead companion in his arms. "Whyyyy!!!!!!!!" he cried to the air above him. "He was so young and innocent! Taken before his time! It's not fair!!" The sword wound that had appeared in Happy's chest, and was spewing blood everywhere, suddenly began to widen. Soon, the gore and entrails the gaping wound was churning out lost its liquid form, and Happy's innards transformed into a brittle powdery substance. Happy's body, once so full of life and vigor, withered away to nothingness, and El Krunko was left cradling his metal-endoskeleton.

El Krunko stood up, and for the first time ever, he began to panic. "There's... There's nothing I can do! What the fuck is going on? Wait a second... My single undoing! All I have to do is..." El Krunko whipped out his Crocodile Dundee Brand Knife ™ and kicked off his ass-stompin' boots.

"Cut it off!" El Krunko rose the knife in the air, and struck downward, but he was too late...

El Krunko's left pinky toe vanished before him, into thin air.

"This does not bode well," he whispered to himself... and that's when he heard it. The sound of Chainsaws revving in the distance.

"Hmm... That doesn't sound like lumberjacks. Oh no! I do believe that's Ancestral Revving!"

El Krunko flipped the throne to its side and hid behind it, while the sounds of the chainsaws grew louder. Soon, El Krunko's heavy breathing and frightened remarks could no longer be heard over the evil chorus of a thousand full throttled Ancestral

Chainsaws that were getting closer.

Could it possibly be!?

TABLET: CCXXXII

El Krunko peered out from behind the throne. Horrors! There, before him, was a sea of El Krunkos, all waving their Ancestral Chainsaws in the air menacingly. "Where are you, El Krunko?" they all intoned in unison, creating a booming chorus of baritone butchers. "We know you are here, now prepare to meet your doom!"

But how? El Krunko wondered. He tried to think of where an army of himself could have come from. His parents? Impossible. Baron Elbert von Krunkhausen and his mistress, Elmira Slagheap, had only two children before they died, Bob the martyr, and El Krunko.

"El Krunko!" the army droned. "Show yourself! There is no escape!"

But El Krunko did not reveal himself just yet. There were more pressing matters on his mind. How could El Krunko possibly defeat an army of himself, particularly when he himself was without an Ancestral Chainsaw, not to mention without the help of his friend and ally Happy Barrypants, who was almost his equal in ass-kickery?

He knelt lower behind the throne, and tears began to fill his eyes.

TABLET: CCXXIII

While cowering miserably in the far corner of the lonely throne room, El Krunko re-lived his life in bitter reflection. *How has El Krunko strayed so far from the true path?* he wondered. *El Krunko was such a happy child. El Krunko wandered free and footlose and fancy free! Free and fancy free El Krunko frolicked fearlessly! None were my equal! Oh happy days of yore!*

The sobs of memories past could not be held back. Like a burst dam, visions of his parents, his extended family, and even Bob the Martyr flooded his mind's eye. But even as they appeared, the images were crushed beneath the boot-heels of a marauding Krunkian horde. He bent over in anguish and pain, and shivered in fetal position like a newborn cub.

Is this what has become of the mighty El Krunko? Family, I have failed thee!

Oh reader, I sense your confusion. All this time we were lead to believe that El Krunko, Lord of the Slay was mightiest of the mighty. The fiercest of the fierce. The caramel in the roast turkey. Now are we to believe that he has fallen to such a lowly foe as an innumerable number of his clones? Of course not! As the army of Ancestral Chainsaw wielding savages marched into the chamber, a flash of bright light blinded everything, before fading into darkness as suddenly as it had come.

"COME OUT EL KRUNKO!" the army cried forth. "MEET YOUR FATE AT THE HANDS OF US! THE MEAN MEAN EL KRUNKLONE TEAM!"

Thousands upon thousands of El Krunkos jumped up and down, and made rude gestures into the darkness.

But then... A small blue light shimmered and glistened in the darkest part of that fateful hour. Appearing before all of them, including El Krunko who was cowering behind the throne, in all his glory, El Krunko appeared!

Only this was no El Krunko, El Krunko had ever seen before.

The El Krunklones blinked in awe.

There before all of them was another El Krunko, bathed in a golden aura, while he floated in mid air above the throne. Little bits of rock and dust shook free of gravity's pull and rose as if some magic force or powerful chi propelled them upwards. El Krunko's mullet grew ten times its normal length, and flew in the air above his head as if it were trying to escape. Waves of heat and light poured from his field of energy, and his rippling muscles sent sonic vibrations out into the Universe. His tender loving eyes were replaced with fierce globes of pure devastation.

The new, improved, El Krunko simply smiled and threw his cloak off, only to reveal his super costume.

TABLET: CCXXIV

Upon his blue spandex uniform was the image of an Ancestral Chainsaw, and when Super El Krunko pulled at the two dimensional portrayal of his treasured weapon, it removed itself from his uniform, and by use of one of his many super powers, turned it into a magical three dimensional manifestation of his A.C. with all of its factory settings restored! There it was, revving in Super El Krunko's hands in all its glory, sharp and shiny as the day it was first manufactured by Ancestro Co. a division of Johnson and Bergstrom Ltd.

Super El Krunko waved his mighty weapon across the room. It hummed like a baby hummingbird, and the El Krunklones were all chopped in twain with a grand blow.

El Krunko stood in astonishment and shock, part of him fearful that this superior version of himself would cut him down next.

But the spandex-clad Super El Krunko merely chuckled, and declared in a manly booming voice, "I know what it is you think, El Krunko, for I myself did think it at one point long ago. You have lost your way, and I am here to set you right."

El Krunko had come face to face with yet another version of himself from a distant, possible future. A scroll appeared in Super El Krunko's hand and he passed it to regular ol' El Krunko, who nearly slipped on the floor, slick as it was with red gore.

El Krunko unfurled it and read – it was a list of tasks!

"Complete these here quests, and the power that I have, and more, will be granted to you by the powers above!"

And by powers above, El Krunko knew this elder version of himself could only mean the all-powerful Author.

"But what of Barry Happypants, and the Mean Mean Monkey Man?" he whined.

"Without this power, you will remain helpless against your foe." Super El Krunko crossed his arms.

El Krunko sighed, shrugged, and nodded in reluctant agreement. He always had found himself a convincing debater.

The heroic Super El Krunko gave his younger self the glistening new Ancestral Chainsaw, for without such a mighty weapon his tasks might prove near-impossible.

"Now go El Krunko, Lord of the Slay, and God of Surfing, to complete the first of your ten Epic quests!" [presented here in summary for the reader at home who does not possess, "The Annotated Songs and Legends of El Krunko," LotS-GoS, first edition. Ed. Gerald V. Smythe. New York: Random House, 6491.]